Caleb

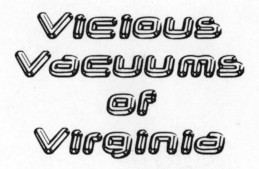

Vicious
Vacuums
of
Virginia

"Ever since you came to my school, everyone has been addicted to your books! My teacher is reading one to us right now, and it's great!"

-Mark F., age 11, Kentucky

"You need to put more pictures of your dogs on your website. I think they're super cute."

-Michelle H., age 12, Oregon

"I have read every one of your American Chillers and Michigan Chillers books. The best one was WICKED VELO-CIRAPTORS OF WEST VIRGINIA. That book gave me nightmares!"

-Erik M., age 9, Florida

"How do you come up with so many cool ideas for your books? You write some really freaky stuff, and that's good."

-Heather G., age 8, Maryland

"I met you at your store, Chillermania, last year. Thanks for signing my books for me! It was the best part of our vacation!"

-David L., age 13, Illinois

"A couple of years ago, I was too young to read your books and they scared me. Now, I love them! I read them every day!"

-Alex P., age 8, Minnesota

"I love your books, and I love to write. My dream is to come to AUTHOR QUEST when I'm old enough. My mom says I can, if I get accepted. I hope I can be a great writer, just like you!"

-Cynthia W., age 8, South Dakota

"Everyone loved it when you came to our school and did an assembly. You were really funny, and we learned a lot about writing and reading."

-Chad R., age 10, Arizona

"You are my favorite author in the whole world! I love every single one of your books!"

-Amy P., age 9, Michigan

"I heard that you wear those weird glasses when you write your books. Is that true? If it is, keep wearing them. Your books are cool!"

-Griffin W., age 12, Maine

"HAUNTING IN NEW HAMPSHIRE is the best ghost story ever! EVER!"

-Kaylee J., age 11, Tennessee

"I don't think anyone else in the world could write as good as you! My favorite book is NEBRASKA NIGHTCRAWL-ERS. Britney is just like me."

-Taylor, M., age 10, Michigan

"I used to hate to read, and now I love it, because of your books. They're really cool! When I read, I pretend that I'm the main character, and I always get freaked out."

-Jack C., age 9, Colorado

Got something cool to say about Johnathan Rand's books? Let us know, and we might publish it right here! Send your short blurb to:
Chiller Blurbs
281 Cool Blurbs Ave.
Topinabee, MI 49791

#30: Vicious Vacuums of Virginia

Johnathan Rand

An AudioCraft Publishing, Inc. book

This book is a work of fiction. Names, places, characters and incidents are used fictitiously, or are products of the author's very active imagination.

No part of this publication may be reproduced in whole or in part, or stored in a retrieval system, or transmitted in any form or by any means, electronic, mechanic, photocopying, recording, or otherwise, without written permission from the publisher. For information regarding permission, write to: AudioCraft Publishing, Inc., PO Box 281, Topinabee Island, MI 49791

American Chillers #30: Vicious Vacuums of Virginia
ISBN 13-digit: 978-1-893699-25-0

Librarians/Media Specialists:
PCIP/MARC records available **free of charge** at
www.americanchillers.com

Cover illustration by Dwayne Harris
Cover layout and design by Sue Harring

Printed in USA

VICIOUS
VACUUMS
OF
VIRGINIA

VISIT CHILLERMANIA!

WORLD HEADQUARTERS FOR BOOKS BY JOHNATHAN RAND!

Visit the HOME for books by Johnathan Rand! Featuring books, hats, shirts, bookmarks and other cool stuff not available anywhere else in the world! Plus, watch the American Chillers website for news of special events and signings at **CHILLERMANIA!** with author Johnathan Rand! Located in northern lower Michigan, on I-75! Take exit 313 . . . then south 1 mile! For more info, call (231) 238-0338. And be afraid! Be veeeery afraaaaaaiiiid . . . .

1

My name is Brooke Whipkey, and I live on Churchside Drive in Gainesville, Virginia, which is a city not far from Washington, D.C. In fact, that's where my mom works. She works at the White House as an assistant for a state senator. She loves her job, but she works late, and she's gone a lot.

My dad is an architect, and he works out of his home office upstairs. He designs homes and buildings, and he's very good at it. He's even won some awards for his designs.

My uncle Chet, who lives only a few miles away, is also very good at what he does: repairing vacuums. He has a shop in a warehouse not far from where we live. He's a nice guy and one of my favorite relatives, but Dad says he's always been a little nutty, that he's always looking for ways to get rich quick. He has some good ideas, but they just never seem to work for him.

But my Uncle Chet's shop was where my friend, Spider Murphy, and I got into a *lot* of trouble. And by the way, his real name isn't 'Spider,' it's Bartholomew. He's named after his great-grandfather, or something like that. But he doesn't like the name, and he doesn't want to be called 'Bart' for short. So, everyone calls him Spider. He said he's been called that ever since he was four years old. Personally, I don't care what anybody's name is. Spider is cool, and he's been a good friend for a long time. We like a lot of the same things, including one hobby in particular:

Electronics.

Now, that might sound strange to you, but not to me. Sure, some of the kids at school think I'm weird. They think I should be more like them.

They don't think of electronics as a hobby that girls should like, but I do. I've loved electronics ever since I was little, when I accidentally received a kit as a gift from my grandparents.

I say 'accidentally' because that's exactly what it was: an accident. You see, my cousin Matt and I share the very same birthday . . . except he's two years older than me and lives in Gainesville, Florida. Well, on my seventh birthday, my grandparents goofed. They sent Matt's present to me in Gainesville, *Virginia* and my present to him in Gainesville, *Florida*. When I opened the box to find an electronics kit, I was really excited. I'd never seen one before, and I thought it was cool. It was very basic, but there were some neat things to build: a homemade radio and a clock that was powered by an ordinary potato! I had a lot of fun.

But the funny part? My grandparents had bought me a talking doll and accidentally sent it to Matt. He was really confused as to why his grandparents would send him a doll.

When my grandparents found out what

they'd done, they felt terrible. The plan was to swap gifts: I would send the electronics kit to Matt, and he would send the doll to me.

But I said no way. I had already opened the electronics kit, and I was having too much fun with it. I didn't even *want* the doll. In the end, Matt gave the doll to his little sister, and my grandparents sent him what he *really* wanted: a skateboard. Everyone was happy . . . especially Matt's little sister, who got a present even though it wasn't her birthday.

But I think I was happiest of all. I had hours of fun with that kit, learning about electricity and how it worked. My parents bought me another kit, and soon I was making all kinds of experimental electrical things on my own. Most of the things I built were pretty basic, but I sure had a lot of fun. I even won first prize at our school science fair when I was only eight years old! It was just a little homemade light bulb, but it was cool and it really worked.

So you see, I've been fascinated with

electrical things for years. I'm still fascinated, of course, but now I tend to be a lot more careful . . . especially after something horrible happened one awful day in December.

When I got home from school that day in December, I was excited to see a package waiting for me. I'd saved up my money and ordered a burglar alarm kit. It was a pretty simple unit, but I thought it would be fun to build it and hook it up to my bedroom door. That way, my brother Andrew would get the surprise of his life the next time he tried to sneak into my room. Andrew is two years younger than me, and he's nothing but a nosy pest. He is always getting into my room, going through my stuff, and just being a pain. I hoped my burglar alarm would catch him in the act.

As far as kits go, my burglar alarm was complicated. I'd already built quite a few electrical things—small, simple robots, lights, radios—things like that. The first ones I built were really easy and were made for beginners.

Since then I've built a lot of things, and I've learned a lot about electricity and how it works. Once, I was able to rewire Mom's broken blinker on her car. She was happy because she said that if she had to take it to the repair shop, it would probably have cost her a fortune.

So, I was always looking for more challenging kits and experiments. After a while, the really simple things get boring. I like challenges, and what I really wanted to do was enter a robotics competition. Not only that, I wanted to *win*. Which, of course, meant that I'd really have to know a lot about electronics.

By building my burglar alarm kit, I was sure

I'd learn a lot. It was designed for kids aged fourteen and older, but I was confident that I could build it even though I was only eleven.

"I'm home, Dad!" I called out as I dropped my book bag on the couch.

"Did you find your package, Brooke?" I heard Dad reply from his upstairs office.

"Yeah!" I said.

"Mom called and said she's going to be late," Dad hollered. "That means I'll be making dinner tonight."

Which meant, of course, that he would call to order a pizza and have it delivered. Dad might be good at designing homes and buildings, but he can't cook worth beans.

But that was fine with me. I love pizza, and so does Andrew.

I picked up the package and carried it to my bedroom. Using my fingernail, I sliced through the packaging tape and carefully opened the box. Inside were the contents of the burglar alarm kit and an instruction booklet.

Spreading out everything on my desk, I got to work, mindful that Andrew would be coming home from soccer practice soon. I didn't want him to see what I was working on, because that would ruin the surprise. After all, the whole purpose in having my burglar alarm was to give him the scare of his life when he came into my bedroom uninvited.

I worked at assembling the alarm. By far, it was the most complicated piece of electronics I'd built. But it was fun.

After working for over an hour, I was almost finished building the alarm. As I inserted the battery, I heard the front door slam. Andrew was home.

I got up to close my bedroom door, so he wouldn't come in when the phone rang. I closed my door behind me, walked into the kitchen, and picked up the phone. It was Spider. He had some questions about his math homework. Spider is pretty smart, but sometimes he just doesn't pay attention. I told him that if he actually listened to our teacher and read his textbooks, he'd be able to figure out the work on his own.

We chatted for a while before I hung up. Andrew had dropped his book bag on the floor and was seated on the couch watching television, and Dad was still upstairs, working. It was four-thirty. In about an hour, he would call down for me to order a large pizza, and Andrew and I would fight over what toppings we wanted.

I walked down the hall and stopped.

Something smelled funny.

I pushed open my bedroom door . . . only to find the entire room filled with smoke!

Panic surged through my entire body. My skin felt hot. My entire room was filled with a cloud of gray smoke.

I quickly saw that the burglar alarm on my desk was the cause. It wasn't on fire, but smoke was rising up, and it looked like it was about to erupt into flames.

Fanning smoke away from my face, I hurried to my desk. Using a screwdriver so I wouldn't burn my fingers, I pried the battery from the unit. I was sure that I had made a mistake in the wiring, and when I had put the battery in, the unit short-circuited.

But now I had another problem.

The smoke had drifted into the hall and set off the smoke alarm. The high-pitched squeal made me jump, and I raced out of my bedroom.

"False alarm, Dad!" I called out. "No need to come downstairs! I'll get it!"

I hurried into the kitchen, grabbed a chair from the dining room table, and carried it into the hall. I stood on it, reached up, and removed the battery from the smoke detector. It immediately ceased its loud, shrill beeping.

I just have to remember to put the battery back in, I thought. To make sure I would remember, I left the chair in the hall and put the battery on it.

Then, I went into my room, closed the door, and opened the window. Cold, wintry air swept in, chilling my skin and swirling the curtains.

Maybe I can get all the smoke smell out before

Dad or Mom or Andrew finds out, I thought hopefully. Not that I would get into any trouble, but there wasn't any need for them to know I could have started the house on fire with my miswired burglar alarm.

Which was another problem. My burglar alarm was fried. The wires were blackened, and the unit's casing was charred. I was sure it was ruined.

I was disappointed, but I realized it could have been much worse. If I'd spent another five minutes talking to Spider, the unit might have burst into flames and set my room on fire. That would have been a disaster.

From that day forward, I decided that whenever it came to electricity, I would be extra careful . . . no matter how simple the project seemed. Electricity isn't something to play around with, and it can be extremely dangerous.

But I never knew how dangerous and terrifying it could be until the following summer at my uncle Chet's vacuum cleaner repair shop.

4

Winter became spring, and spring turned into summer. School let out. I turned twelve on June fifteenth and had a fun birthday party. I got a lot of cool presents, including a super-cool solar powered fan kit.

By then, I'd learned a lot more about robotics and electronics. I went to the hobby store whenever I had the money to buy another kit.

And that became a problem, because kits cost money. Some of them can be really expensive, too.

So, I started to look for ways to earn money. I had a lemonade stand, but there aren't many people that go by our block, and I didn't earn very much. I tried a dog walking service, but I got only a few customers. Most people who own dogs like to walk with their pets.

I even made flyers and took them around to houses, advertising babysitting services. I posted my flyers on telephone poles and slid them under car windshields. But I didn't get any work, and I think it was because not many people want to hire a twelve-year old babysitter.

One weekend, Spider and I knocked on doors, offering to wash cars. We got a little bit of business, but not much. We washed two cars and made ten dollars.

"Why don't you call my brother?" Dad suggested one day. "He might have something you can do at his shop."

"Uncle Chet?" I asked.

"Sure," Dad said. "He doesn't have any other

employees at his repair shop. Last time I was there, it was a mess. He never cleans or organizes anything. You might be able to do some work for him."

"That's a great idea!" I said. "I'll go ask him right now!"

I raced to the garage and hopped on my bike. Uncle Chet's shop is about two miles from where we live, so it didn't take me long to get there. I turned into the parking lot, cruised up to the front of the building and stopped, glancing up at the large sign above a big, plate glass window.

Gainesville Vacuum Repair
No Vacuum Too Small
Free Estimates

The building was an old warehouse made of metal. It originally was white, but time and weather had caused it to become a chalky gray color. It sat empty for years, until Uncle Chet bought it. He had originally started his business in his garage, but quickly outgrew it and needed a bigger place. The warehouse was huge—much bigger than his garage—but he said that if his business continued to grow, he would need all of the space and maybe more. As it was, the building was as big as our school gymnasium. I couldn't imagine an entire gymnasium filled with old, used vacuums.

But, if I couldn't imagine that, I would never be able to imagine what was waiting for me inside.

I pushed open the front door. A couple of brass bells dangling from a string on the inside of the door jangled against the glass as I stepped inside.

Dad was right, I thought. *This place is a mess.*

There were dozens of old appliances—vacuum cleaners, mostly—in the front room, which also served as a small store. The building had been divided, and this space—the front office and store—was small, the size of a two-car garage. At the back of the room was a door that opened into the workshop and main warehouse, where Uncle Chet stored all of the vacuum cleaners that couldn't be fixed. He never threw them out, because he said he could always use them for spare parts.

But his front store and office was a different story. There were used vacuums in all shapes and sizes lining the floor. There were shelves on the wall with small, handheld vacuums lined up like books. There were a few other appliances mixed in, too—old toasters, mixers, and some power tools. But for the most part, it was wall-to-wall vacuum cleaners.

And there was no sign of my uncle.

"Uncle Chet?" I called out.

There was no reply.

Where did he go? I wondered. *Why would he leave his shop empty, with the door unlocked?*

The answer, of course, was that he wouldn't. He had to be around, and he was most likely in the bigger warehouse in back.

"Uncle Chet?" I called out once more, a bit

louder this time. "It's me, Brooke."

When I still heard nothing, I made my way through the room, weaving around a thick nest of vacuum cleaners. Most had tags with prices, and some had tags that read *Sold.* There was a layer of dust on some of them, and I noticed that there was also dust and small debris on the floor . . . mainly small pieces of wire or plastic.

Uncle Chet could sure use some help cleaning this place, I thought. *It would be great if he would hire me.*

But first, I'd have to find him.

I reached the back door and hesitated. A black sign with orange letters read *PRIVATE - KEEP OUT.*

I knocked. "Uncle Chet?"

Waited.

Listened.

Leaning forward, I placed my ear against the door. I could hear the hum of a vacuum coming from inside the big warehouse.

That's where he is, all right, I thought. *I'll just*

poke my head in and let him know I'm here.

I grasped the knob. It was cold and a little greasy. Turning it, I pushed the door open and poked my head inside.

"Uncle Ch—"

I froze and stopped speaking, horrified by the sight of my uncle, face down on the floor.

For a moment, I just stared.

Uncle Chet was sprawled on the floor, face down. He was wearing dark blue pants and a light blue shirt, and his curly black hair was messy. His arms were spread out, and one of his legs was bent. A grease-stained red toolbox sat near his right hand. The lid was open, and there were several hand tools on the floor.

Next to the toolbox, an old upright vacuum cleaner snarled—and I mean *snarled*. It was running, but the noise it created sounded low and unnatural, not anything like the way a vacuum cleaner should sound. It wasn't very loud, either, and as I looked at it, one word popped into my head.

Alive, I thought. *It's like the thing is alive.*

Quickly, I came to my senses. *Vacuum cleaners aren't alive, Brooke. Whatever is going on, Uncle Chet needs help.*

I pushed open the door and rushed into the warehouse. The first thing I did was find the power switch on the vacuum cleaner and turn it off. Then, I knelt next to my uncle and heard another sound.

Snoring.

I could see the slight rise and fall of his back as he breathed.

Is he sleeping? I wondered. *Did he fall asleep, or did he fall?*

I looked around. I didn't see any blood, no evidence of anything he'd tripped over.

I put my hand on his shoulder and shook

him gently.

"Uncle Chet?" I whispered. *"Uncle Chet?"*

His arm moved, and he began to stir.

"Uncle Chet? It's me. Brooke. Your niece. Are you all right?"

Uncle Chet lifted his head.

"Yeah," he said, sounding disoriented.

"Are you all right?" I repeated.

"Sure," he replied, slowly propping himself up on his elbows. Then, he rolled to his side and got to his knees. He looked at me and scratched his head.

"How did you get inside?" he asked.

"Through the front door," I replied.

"Oh," he said absently. "I must've forgot to lock it. I always lock it when it's time for my nap."

"You were taking a nap?" I asked.

Uncle Chet nodded. "I've been working a lot lately," he said, running a hand through his disheveled mop of hair. "Lots of late nights. I've got a special project I've been working on, and it's keeping me busy. Sometimes it's just quicker to get in forty winks here, rather than go home."

"Yeah, I guess so," I said, trying to sound like I understood. But I still thought it was weird. I mean . . . whoever heard of taking a nap face down on the floor of a dirty warehouse? He could at least bring a cot or maybe a couch to work. That would be a lot more comfortable. Of course, Dad did tell me that Uncle Chet has always been a little odd. Smart, but odd.

"Whatcha need?" Uncle Chet said as he got to his feet. "A vacuum cleaner? Something you need fixed?"

I shook my head. "No," I said. "I need a job."

Uncle Chet frowned. "A job?" he said.

"Yeah," I replied. "I need a job, so I can earn some money."

Uncle Chet stroked the grainy, dark film of razor stubble on his chin. He looked like he hadn't shaved in a couple of days. "A job," he mused. "Hmmm. You just had a birthday, right?"

I nodded. "Yes. I just turned twelve last month."

"What do you need the money for?" he asked.

"So I can buy more electronic kits from the hobby store," I replied.

Uncle Chet thought about this. He stroked his chin again and looked around the warehouse. I followed his gaze, looking at the mass of old vacuum cleaners littering the enormous room. And I say 'littering,' because that's what it looked like: a giant warehouse filled with litter. I'd never seen so many old and broken vacuums.

Still, I knew that when it came to repairing them, Uncle Chet was a genius. He was keeping all of this junk around for some reason, probably for spare parts. Dad told me once that there wasn't a vacuum cleaner in Virginia that Uncle Chet couldn't fix, and I believed it.

"Okay, you're hired," he said.

I blinked once. Twice. I was stunned.

"I am?" I asked.

"Sure," he replied. "You can start right now." He pointed to the vacuum that had been running while he was sleeping, the one I had shut off. "Fix that one right there. The customer is going to be here later today to pick it up. After you fix that one, the small handheld vacuum next to it needs to be looked at."

Fix vacuum cleaners? Was he serious?

I was about to protest, to tell him that I wanted a job *cleaning,* not *repairing.* Sure, I was getting pretty good at electronics, but I'd never repaired a vacuum cleaner. Once, at home, I took our vacuum cleaner apart and put it back together. But that was because I wanted to see how it worked.

Then again, I thought, *I might as well give it a shot. It's a job. A job means money. Maybe I can fix it, after all.*

"I'll get right to work," I said confidently, placing my hand on the vacuum cleaner's handle. "But why would you take a nap and leave this running?"

Uncle Chet stared at me, puzzled. "Running?" he replied. "I didn't leave it running."

"Yes, you did," I said, nodding. "When I came through the door, you were on the floor, and the vacuum cleaner was on. And it sounded weird."

My uncle looked at the vacuum. "Hmph," he grunted. "Well, there have been a lot of weird things going on lately."

Weird things? I thought. *What kind of weird things?*

But before I could ask him about it, he had left the warehouse and returned to the front office, leaving me to wonder:

If he didn't turn on the vacuum cleaner, then who did? Vacuum cleaners don't turn on by themselves.

And at that very moment, that's exactly what the appliance did. There was a soft clicking sound, and the vacuum cleaner whirred to life . . . *all by itself!*

I wanted to turn and run, and I almost did. I was horrified—I think anyone would be—and I wanted out of the warehouse, away from the vacuum as fast as my legs could carry me.

But a couple of things stopped me. If I ran screaming to my uncle, he would think I was crazy. There's no way he would believe that the vacuum cleaner turned on all by itself. He'd fire me and tell me to go home, and I'd lose my job.

And I knew that vacuum cleaners don't turn

on by themselves. There had to be a reason. Vacuum cleaners aren't alive any more than a power drill or a refrigerator.

There's something wrong that is making it turn on, I thought, trying to remain calm. *There's something wrong with the wiring, some internal problem that's causing it to malfunction.*

That didn't explain the strange sound it was making, which was a low, gurgling snarl like I'd heard when I first came into the warehouse. I had to admit, it sounded creepy. If a vacuum cleaner could growl, that was what it was doing.

"Nonsense," I said out loud to no one. "Vacuum cleaners don't turn on by themselves."

I took a deep breath, strode over to the appliance, and turned it off.

Nothing happened.

The switch was in the 'off' position, but the unit was still on, still making that same, angry snarling sound.

I flipped the switch up and down, but nothing happened. The motor continued to run.

Well, then, I thought, *I'll just unplug it. It won't be able to run if it's not plugged into an electrical outlet.*

I stepped behind the vacuum and found the cord. It was dark gray, and it snaked along the floor around other vacuums toward the wall. I followed it until I found where it was plugged into the outlet. I grabbed it and was just about to pull, when I heard another sound.

A soft grinding.

Now what? I wondered.

Instead of unplugging the cord, I stood and turned around . . . only to find the vacuum cleaner moving by itself, stalking me!

I was frozen in sheer terror, but not for long. I wasn't just going to stand there while the evil appliance came after me.

I turned, knelt down, grasped the power cord, and yanked it from the electrical outlet. The vacuum's motor stopped and quickly faded, and the unit stopped moving.

I stood still for a moment, holding the cord in my hand, staring at the vacuum cleaner. It was an ordinary household appliance, but it had taken on a dark, sinister look. The single light at the base looked like a probing eye, glaring at me, watching me, waiting for my next move. The oblong dust bag behind the handle was a bloated stomach, filled with whatever the vacuum had eaten. Even the base of the unit seemed to resemble a jaw with teeth, ready to chomp any prey in its path.

You're being ridiculous, Brooke, I thought. *Stop letting your imagination run wild and get to work. The vacuum isn't alive, it's just not working right. The first thing I need to do is find out what's wrong.*

I turned and plugged the cord into the wall, expecting the machine to begin running again, but it didn't.

Weird.

Although I didn't have much experience with vacuum cleaners, I was certain I knew enough to begin taking it apart. The first thing I was going to look at was the on and off switch. It seemed like the most logical place to start.

I unplugged the appliance from the electrical

outlet, so I wouldn't get shocked—or worse. Like I said before: you don't fool around with electricity. It can be deadly.

I returned to the vacuum cleaner. Upon closer inspection, I discovered that it was self-propelled. We used to have a vacuum cleaner like that. When you pushed it forward, an internal motor turned on and rotated the wheels, driving the appliance. The same thing happened when you pulled it toward you. This took some of the work out of pushing and pulling the vacuum all over the house.

Which, of course, explained why the vacuum appeared to be coming after me.

But they can't turn on all by themselves, I reminded myself.

I reached into Uncle Chet's toolbox, found a screwdriver, and got to work. In less than a minute, I had the vacuum's upper housing removed and discovered the problem: the wires connected to the power switch were old and frayed and were touching. That would mean the power would be interrupted, and the vacuum would shut off. Or, if the unit was off, the machine could turn on anytime the wires came in contact with one another.

It was an easy fix. I simply found another vacuum cleaner that was beyond repair—which was easy to do, because there were hundreds in the warehouse. I found a unit that had wires similar to the vacuum I was working on. I removed the old, frayed wires and replaced them. Then, I returned the plastic housing to the base of the handle and tightened the screws.

I also found that the belt that powered the motor brush was old and rotting, which was causing the strange snarling sound. I replaced it with another belt I swiped from another used vacuum.

Now, the test. I needed to plug the power cord into the wall to see if it worked. I put the screwdriver on the floor, picked up the cord, turned, knelt down, and was about to plug the cord into the wall.

A sudden noise stopped me and I spun, losing my balance and nearly falling over.

The vacuum cleaner was on . . . and it wasn't even plugged in!

I turned and stared, letting the power cord dangle from my hand.

A vacuum was running, all right . . . but it wasn't the vacuum I had been working on. It was the smaller, handheld unit—the one Uncle Chet had asked me to work on next.

Now, how could that one turn on by itself? I wondered. *It's operated by a rechargeable battery. Could it have the same problem as the one I just worked on?*

I dropped the cord, walked to where the small vacuum was, and picked it up. The button was in the 'on' position, and I switched it off. The whining motor died.

I looked at it carefully as I flipped it over in my hands. The appliance wasn't quite as long as my arm. The housing was a light brown color, and the snout was a smoky, transparent plastic.

The problem, I discovered, was the unit had a crack in the bottom right corner, which was the battery housing. I popped the cover off and found that the rechargeable battery was dented. The vacuum had probably been dropped, and the force of the blow had jammed the battery connection—meaning that while the vacuum was in the 'on' position, it would work only once in a while. I assumed Uncle Chet had turned it on, but it hadn't worked. He probably left the switch in that position when he put it aside, and the unit had seemingly turned on by itself. If I hadn't turned it off, it probably would have turned itself off sooner or later or simply run out of juice.

The warehouse door opened, and Uncle Chet came in.

"I just sold a vacuum," he said, pumping a fist in the air. "That's the fourth one today."

I smiled. "Great," I said.

"How's it going in here?" he asked.

"Good, I think," I said. I pointed to the upright vacuum next to me. "I think I fixed this one," I continued. Then, I raised the handheld unit. "But the battery housing on this one is cracked. I think it can be glued, but it's probably going to need a new battery connection."

"I'm sure we'll be able to find a spare laying around here somewhere," Uncle Chet said. "But I just don't know where I'm going to get the time to fix all of the vacuums waiting to get repaired. I'd rather spend the time working on my new invention."

"What's that?" I asked.

Uncle Chet grinned like a clever cat. "I'll show you," he replied. "But it's top-secret. No one can know about this. If I'm successful, I'll be a millionaire."

"Wow," I said, remembering what Dad had always told me: *Uncle Chet had always been a little nutty, always looking for ways to get rich quick.*

"Follow me," he said, "and I'll show you."

I placed the handheld vacuum on the floor and followed Uncle Chet as he wove through the maze of vacuum cleaners. There were so many that he'd created a path, a thin trail through a forest of vacuums. Most of them were old, dating back dozens of years. A few were newer . . . but all had something wrong with them. They were packed haphazardly in the warehouse like they had been tossed there. Many were on their sides with wires hanging out.

At the far end of the warehouse, we came to a door.

"Nobody knows I built this wall," he said with a wink. "I don't want anyone to know I have a private, secret workshop."

I smiled, wondering who on earth would know.

And who on earth would care? I thought.

He pulled a knotted wad of keys from his pocket, and I saw that there were not one, not two, but *three* locks on the door, in addition to the locking doorknob. Uncle Chet was really serious about keeping people out.

He carefully inserted separate keys into each of the locks. There was a loud clunking sound every time he turned a key. Finally, he inserted a key into the doorknob. He turned and looked at me with that catlike grin again.

"Don't be afraid, and don't get freaked out," he said.

What a strange thing to say, I thought. *What could possibly be on the other side of that door that would frighten me or freak me out?*

But then he opened the door, and I realized that Dad was wrong. Uncle Chet wasn't a little nutty . . . he had gone totally and completely *crazy.*

Uncle Chet walked into his secret workshop, but I didn't follow. I could only stand and stare.

I was wrong, I thought. *Because I'm freaked out. I'm freaked out, and I'm frightened.*

I was freaked out by what I saw in the room, but I was more frightened by the fact that, truly, my uncle had gone starkraving mad. A lunatic.

When he realized I wasn't following him into his workshop, he turned and looked at me. He was still smiling, and his eyes shined.

"What do you think?" he said, spreading his arms wide.

I looked around the room, trying to take in what I was seeing.

The room was clean. Spotless, in fact. High above, hanging from the ceiling, tubes of white fluorescent lights illuminated the entire workshop. The floor was made of shiny, cream-colored tile.

And there were twelve beds, side by side, in the middle of the room. On each bed lay a vacuum cleaner, each one connected to a series of wires and cables that connected to a large, computer-like shelf of apparatus standing next to each bed.

It's like a hospital, I thought. *It's like an operating room for vacuum cleaners, and my uncle is the crazy doctor. A mad scientist.*

I found the courage to walk through the doorway and into the room. I was freaked out, but I was also curious.

"What . . . what in the world *is* all this stuff?" I stammered. "What are you doing in here?"

"This is my secret workshop," Uncle Chet

replied. "No one knows about it. You're the first."

I frowned. "Yes, but what am I looking at? What is all this stuff?"

"It's a project I've been working on for over a year," Uncle Chet replied. "Fully computerized, battery-powered vacuum cleaners that work all by themselves."

"Fully computerized?" I said.

Uncle Chet nodded and walked to one of the beds. I followed him and realized that they weren't beds after all, but tables. Each was covered with a clean white tablecloth, making it appear like a bed.

"I've implanted each vacuum with its own computer motherboard, along with a tiny radio receiver. Each vacuum can be programmed remotely from its own mainframe." He pointed to a computer keyboard on the table. "After they're programmed, the vacuum cleaners work all by themselves without any help from humans."

"Kind of like those disc vacuums," I said. "The ones that scoot around on the floor all by themselves."

Uncle Chet's eyes lit up. "Exactly!" he said. "Only my vacuums can be remotely programmed and are much more powerful, designed for deep cleaning. I've made the intake much bigger for more effective cleaning. See?"

He dragged his finger along the base, outlining the large intake.

"It'll be a household miracle!" he continued. "Think about it: people will be able to program their own vacuum cleaners to clean at a certain time of the day, even if they're not home. The vacuum cleaner will do all the work."

I looked at the row of upright vacuums laying on their sides on the white tables, connected to the wires and cables. Each appliance reminded me of humans in hospital beds. It was eerie.

"I'm stuck on one problem, though," Uncle Chet said, scratching his head.

"What's that?" I asked.

"Stairs," he said. "None of the vacuums can climb stairs. If I could only figure that out, then my invention would be complete. I'll make millions."

I looked at the vacuum cleaner on the table in front of me.

I looked closer.

Closer still.

An idea began to take shape. Uncle Chet noticed how deep in thought I was and spoke.

"What?" he asked curiously. "What are you thinking?"

I'm thinking about everything Spider and I know about robotics, I thought. *We can create automated arms and legs on these things, and the vacuums will be able to climb stairs.*

"Brooke?" Uncle Chet said.

I put my hands on my hips. "I think I can solve your problem," I said. "But I'm going to need help from a friend. He's cool, and he can keep quiet and not tell anyone."

"Okay," Uncle Chet said.

"And if it works, we'll want a cut of your millions," I said, folding my arms across my chest.

Uncle Chet flinched. I don't think he was used to a twelve-year old asking to be part of a huge business deal.

"Fair enough," he said. "I'll draw up the paperwork."

We shook hands and sealed the deal.

I'm going to be a millionaire, too, I thought. *So is Spider Murphy. We're going to be rich and famous.*

I looked at all the vacuums on the tables, and once again the images reminded me of humans, sleeping peacefully in their hospital beds.

We can do this, I thought. *We can make these things operate all by themselves. We can make mechanical legs that will allow the appliances to climb up and down stairs and even over small tables and other objects. It will be like they have a mind of their own.*

At the time, that thought wasn't frightening.

A mind of their own.

In fact, it was an exciting thought.

All by themselves.

A mind of their own.

That's the trouble with big ideas. If you

succeed, the rewards are enormous.

But if you fail, the price can often be disastrous. Very soon, we would be paying that price . . . in a horrifying way.

When I left the warehouse and Uncle Chet's secret workshop later that day, I rode over to Spider's house. Now, we were sitting on his porch, sipping lemonade. His cat, Gizmo, sat next to him. Gizmo was a stray that showed up at the Murphy's front door two years ago. He was all gray with a white splotch on his nose. Spider made flyers and posted them around the neighborhood, trying to find the cat's owner. Two weeks later when he hadn't found the animal's home, he convinced his parents to let him keep him. He named him Gizmo, saying that the cat looked like a Gizmo.

"You want me to help you do *what?*" Spider asked. I had just told him what my Uncle Chet had been working on, the problem he had with the vacuums, and how I thought we could help find a solution.

"Think about it," I said. "You and I know a lot about robotics. We've built all sorts of robots from kits. I'm sure we can find a way to connect legs to the vacuum cleaners—legs that would allow the vacuums to climb up and down stairs, even over tables and chairs. And Uncle Chet is going to give us a cut of the money he earns. What do you think?"

"I think it's a cool idea," Spider replied warily. "But do these vacuums work?"

"What do you mean?" I asked.

"Did you actually see one of these vacuums in action?"

I frowned. *No, I hadn't,* I thought. *I never asked Uncle Chet to see one of his special, battery-*

powered self-operating vacuums in action.

I shook my head. "No," I replied. "I didn't ask."

"Don't you think we should find out if they work first?" Spider continued. "I mean . . . his idea sounds a little far-fetched, don't you think? Vacuums that can be programmed by a computer to run on their own?"

"Yeah," I agreed. "But you've got to know my Uncle Chet. He's smart."

"Doesn't he know anything about robotics?" Spider asked.

I shook my head. "Not as much as we do. He said he could probably figure it out himself, but it would take time. He's in a hurry to get this invention finished so it can be perfected and he can make his millions."

"And we get a share of that?" Spider asked.

"Yeah," I said.

Spider sipped his lemonade and fell silent, deep in thought.

"Okay," he said finally. "Let's do it. But first,

I want to see one of those vacuums. I want to see if they really *do* what your uncle says they can do."

"He's there, now," I said. "Let's go to his shop and talk to him.

We rode our bikes to the big warehouse. Uncle Chet was in the front office, speaking with a customer. As we arrived the customer left, carrying a large, upright vacuum. I realized it was the vacuum I had worked on earlier in the day. Although I hadn't had a chance to test it, my repairs must have worked.

"Hi, Uncle Chet," I said as we walked inside. "This is my friend, Spider. I told him all about your secret project."

"I promise not to say a word to anyone," Spider said.

"Good," Uncle Chet said. "Brooke said you could be trusted."

"Spider wants to see one of your special vacuums work," I said. "He wants to see how it can be programmed."

Uncle Chet nodded. "Follow me," he said.

We strode through the back door and made our way through the wasteland of old vacuum cleaners. Spider's head turned from side to side as he walked.

"I can't believe how many vacuums are in here," he whispered.

When we reached the door to the secret workshop, Uncle Chet went through the same routine of unlocking all the locks, then unlocking the doorknob.

I smiled. "Wait until you see this," I said to Spider.

Uncle Chet pushed the door open and walked into the workshop.

Suddenly, a motor roared to life. Uncle Chet turned to the right. Caught by surprise, his eyes flew open. He leapt back and threw his hands up to protect himself, but it was too late. The vacuum cleaner was upon him, knocking him to the ground, where it began to gnaw at his leg!

The appliance had been waiting behind the door for just the right moment, and Uncle Chet was caught completely off guard by the ambush. When he walked into his workshop, the vacuum attacked. The intake underneath the base had become a hungry, ravenous mouth, and it was chomping and chewing at Uncle Chet's leg.

Without even thinking about the danger, I raced to help. I grabbed the vacuum cleaner's handle and pulled. I succeeded for a moment, but the vacuum's suction was incredibly strong. That's when I realized it didn't have a mouth, and that it wasn't chewing on my uncle's leg. The powerful suction had caught the bottom portion of his pants, and it was sucking the material into the machine.

"Spider, help!" I shouted.

Spider raced to my side. Together, we were able to pull the appliance from Uncle Chet.

"Don't let it go!" Uncle Chet said as he ran to an empty table.

Meanwhile, the vacuum that Spider and I held struggled to get away. It was incredibly strong, and it took both of us to keep it from forcing itself from our grasp.

I found the power switch and flicked it to the 'off' position, but it had no effect. The vacuum's motor continued to roar, and the machine kept trying to pull away from us.

Uncle Chet was tapping furiously at a keyboard next to the table, looking at a computer monitor on top of the electrical unit.

"There," he said. "I've overridden its internal

programming."

The motor died instantly, fading away in seconds.

Spider and I let go of the handle.

"Well," Spider said, "at least we know they work."

Uncle Chet walked toward us. "There are still a few bugs I've got to work out," he said. "I'm still having problems with the programming, and some of the vacuums are doing weird things. But I'm getting close. When can you guys get started?"

I looked at Spider, and he looked at me.

"How about tomorrow?" I said.

Spider nodded. "Yeah, I can get started tomorrow. Nine o'clock?"

"Fine," Uncle Chet said with a smile. "Tomorrow morning at nine. It will be an historical event!"

Yeah, it was going to be an historical event, all right . . . for all the wrong reasons.

I ordered an extra large pizza that night. Dad, Andrew, and I ate while watching television. Mom came home late, and when she came into my bedroom to say good-night, she was munching on a piece of pizza. I told her that Uncle Chet had hired me to help fix vacuums.

"You amaze me, Brooke," she said. "Other girls are interested in soccer, clothes, books, or movies. You're interested in electronics."

"You think that's bad?" I asked.

Mom shook her head. "Not at all," she said. "It's what makes you unique and special. I was a little different when I was your age and other kids thought I was strange, but I didn't care. It's important to be yourself. What other people think doesn't matter."

The next morning, I was the first one up. I stumbled into the kitchen and opened the refrigerator door. I found a couple of leftover pieces of pizza, so I ate them for breakfast. Then, I went into the living room and turned on the television, clicking through the channels. It was pretty much the same old thing I saw every day: news, sports, and cartoons. The weather lady said that it was going to rain all day in Gainesville and that we might even get a thunderstorm.

A great day to be indoors working on those vacuum cleaners, I thought as I turned off the television. Then, I went into my room and changed into a pair of old jeans and a T-shirt: things that wouldn't matter if they got dirty. I'd be taking apart vacuum cleaners all day, so I was bound to get grime and grease on myself.

It was still early, so I read for a while. The book was about dolls that came to life in Delaware, and it was pretty freaky. I wondered how on earth anyone could come up with such a bizarre story.

When Mom and Dad got up, I went into the kitchen and talked with them while they sipped coffee. My brother Andrew was still sleeping.

"Ready for your first day on the job?" Dad asked.

"Yeah," I said. "It's going to be fun." Although I had told Mom and Dad I was working for Uncle Chet, I didn't tell them I was working on his secret project. Oh, I didn't lie to them. I just thought that it would be a great surprise when they found out that Spider and I had played a big part in a great new invention. They'd be proud.

And if we made a bunch of money? Even better.

Rich and famous, I thought.

Now, I'd like to say that all of the horrifying things that were about to happen had nothing to do with us. I'd like to say that we weren't responsible for any of it. I'd like to blame it on someone or something else, maybe blame it on the thunderstorm.

But that wasn't true. It was *all* our fault. Everything that happened was a direct result of what Spider and I did. If we hadn't been in Uncle Chet's secret workshop, nothing would have happened. Most certainly, the vacuums wouldn't have come alive.

And when I say 'alive,' I mean *alive*. These weren't just mechanical robots, programmed by humans to do basic tasks. These things were alive and acted on their own . . . and we were going to find out really quick that they didn't like humans.

It stopped raining around eight, but the sky remained dark and gray. The street was shiny and wet, and water dripped from leaves and tree branches. A few puddles had formed in our driveway.

At eight-thirty, I put my raincoat in my backpack, slipped it on, and rode my bike to Spider's house. He was waiting for me on the porch. His bike was leaning against a tree, and Gizmo was sitting in the grass, eyeing a blue jay on a feeder that dangled from a branch. The cat's tail swished slowly back and forth like a willow in a gentle breeze.

"Right on time," he said with a smile. He stood and hopped onto his bike. "At least the rain quit."

I looked into the gray sky. "Not for long," I said. "It's supposed to rain all day."

"Well, let's get to your uncle's before it starts again," Spider said.

In minutes, we were rolling into the parking lot of Uncle Chet's shop. His car was parked near the front entrance, and we went inside and found him sitting behind the cash register, sorting a pile of papers and receipts.

"You guys are right on time," he said, glancing out the window. "Good thing. Looks like the rain is starting again."

It was. I'd noticed a few sprinkles when we'd reached the parking lot, and now it was drizzling harder, creating streaks on the windows.

"Bring your bikes inside," Uncle Chet said.

"That way, I can keep an eye on them, and they'll be out of the rain."

Spider and I wheeled our bikes in and leaned them against a wall.

"You guys ready to get to work?" my uncle asked.

We nodded. "I am," I said.

"Me, too," Spider echoed.

"I think you'll find all the tools you need back there," he said, hiking his thumb toward the door that led to the warehouse and workshop. "And you can use any parts you want from any of those old vacuum cleaners. Which reminds me: the top hinges on the door to my workshop are loose, and I haven't had a chance to fix them yet. Don't push too hard when you open the door."

"Gotcha," I said.

"You guys really think you can do this?" my uncle asked. "You really think you can add legs to those vacuums and make them work?"

"Yeah," I said. "I think we can. We might have to do some experimenting, but I think we can make it work."

"Terrific!" Uncle Chet said as he wrung his hands together. "I'm going to be rich. We all will be. You guys will be the richest kids in Virginia!"

I must admit, that was an enticing thought. But I was also excited about working with the wires and tools. I liked the feel of the materials in my hands, the idea that I was creating something unique, new, and different. And this time, unlike the robotic kits we'd put together, we would be making something to benefit other people. Customers who bought our vacuum cleaners would save time and energy, because the appliance would be doing the work for them.

"You guys can head on back," Uncle Chet said. "I've got a lot of work to do up here. I've already unlocked the door for you."

"Great," I said. "We'll work until lunchtime, then take a break."

Uncle Chet's eyes lit up. "That reminds me," he said. "I'll order some sandwiches and have them delivered at noon. When they get here, I'll bring them back to you."

"Cool," Spider said.

"Yeah, thanks," I said.

We left the front office and made our way through the piles of old vacuums in the warehouse.

"It must have taken your uncle years to collect all these things," Spider said as we approached the door to Uncle Chet's secret workshop.

"I think he's been repairing vacuum cleaners since he was in high school," I said. "He's been—"

Spider stopped. He'd been walking in front of me, and I bumped into him.

"What was that?" he asked.

"What was what?" I replied, peering over his shoulder.

"*I heard something,*" he whispered.

We listened for a moment. The only thing I could hear was the faint drumming of the rain on the metal roof of the warehouse.

"I don't hear anything," I said.

"I heard something," Spider insisted.

Then, ahead of us, we *did* hear something.

A creaking sound.

The door to Uncle Chet's secret laboratory was slowly opening.

"Maybe this isn't a good idea, after all," Spider whispered.

We watched as the door continued to move, seemingly all by itself. When it was halfway open, it stopped.

"It's got to be that loose hinge my uncle told us about," I said. "The door is unbalanced, that's all. Come on. We'll fix it for him."

I took one step, and stopped. In the doorway to Uncle Chet's secret laboratory, an upright vacuum cleaner appeared. It hummed softly as it rolled to a stop.

Then, the appliance roared to life and hurled itself at us like it had been shot out of a cannon!

Spider dove to the right, and I leapt to the left, tripping on a small vacuum. I went down, crashing into several machines and knocking them over.

The upright vacuum sped past us and finally crashed into a bunch of old units. It tumbled to the side, its small wheels spinning. Motor roaring, it shuddered and shook on the floor as if it was attempting to right itself.

Spider grabbed an old vacuum and pushed it in front of him, as if to use it as a shield. I brushed aside some of the old vacuums that had toppled onto me and got to my feet. I turned and ran past Spider, into the secret workshop where the rest of the vacuums rested on their tables. I ran to the empty table, my eyes darting to the electrical unit and the computer monitor next to it.

How do I shut that thing off? I wondered. My mind was frantic as I looked at the monitor and the computer keyboard on the table. *I know they're remotely programmed through a radio of some sort, but how do I shut the vacuum down?*

"It's still trying to get up!" Spider shouted from the other room.

"I'm trying to figure this out!" I shouted back.

The computer screen was blank. I hit the *Enter* key, and it blinked to life. A list of options glowed in black letters. I scrolled through until I found what I was looking for:

SYSTEM SHUTDOWN

I highlighted the words and hit the *Enter* key.

"What's it doing now?" I shouted.

"I think it stopped," Spider replied. "It's not wiggling around anymore, and the motor quit running."

I left the table, walked through the bright workshop, and into the storage area. Spider was slowly walking toward the vacuum that had attacked, wary that it might leap up and attack again.

"What did you do?" he asked, his eyes never leaving the vacuum cleaner in front of him.

"There's a system shutdown option on the computer," I said. "That's good to know, especially if some of these things start going crazy."

"Well," Spider said, "like your uncle told us: he still doesn't have all of the bugs worked out. Inventions like this take experimentation and time. I don't think Thomas Edison invented a perfect light bulb on his first try."

Outside, the rain fell harder, and the drops hitting the metal roof became a dull roar. Thunder rumbled.

I walked to the fallen vacuum cleaner, knelt down, and looked closely. Some of my uncle's modifications made the vacuum look oddly robot-like. For instance, the rolling brush at the base now had hard wire brushes that resembled teeth. There were two small cones, like little satellite dishes, that looked like ears. The plastic lens covering the single light looked like a single, leering eye. All of these changes and modifications made the appliance appear lifelike, as if it were some sort of robotic animal from the future.

"The first thing we're going to have to do is keep those things from running around on their own," Spider said. "Nobody is going to want an out-of-control vacuum cleaner."

"I don't think it'll be too hard to fix," I said. "If we can't, I'm sure Uncle Chet will be able to. Our job is to give the vacuums more mobility, so they can go up and down stairs. I think we'll be able to do that."

There was no doubt in my mind that we

would be able to perfect Uncle Chet's invention. I was certain we would be able to attach moveable legs to give the appliance the ability to climb stairs.

But, as we would soon discover, the appliances had their own ideas about what they were going to do.

I righted the vacuum cleaner, pushed it into Uncle Chet's secret workshop, and placed it on the table. Spider followed me, and the two of us looked at the row of vacuums connected to electric wires and cables.

"Strange," Spider said. "How did the vacuum get off the table by itself?"

"I don't know," I replied. "Maybe it was close to the edge, and the vibration was enough to make it fall off the side."

"But how did it get turned on?" Spider asked.

I shrugged.

"Beats me," I replied. "But they're only appliances, powered by batteries and a computer. It's not like they're alive. I worked on one yesterday that turned on and off all by itself. It just had a short circuit in the wiring. Come on. Let's get to work."

The first thing we did was take apart one of the vacuum cleaners to see how we would connect the moveable legs. Then, we started sketching designs of how the legs would look, what we would make them out of, and how to assemble and attach them to the units. This was probably the most important part, because there were so many possibilities. My mind was constantly thinking about Thomas Edison. He'd invented many things: the phonograph, the motion picture camera, and the light bulb, among many, many other inventions. In fact, it was Thomas Edison who said that 'Genius is one percent inspiration, and ninety-nine percent perspiration.' Meaning that to invent anything, you have to put in a lot of time and effort. You don't build a rocket overnight . . . and you don't add mechanical legs to self-propelled, battery-powered vacuum cleaners in an hour or two.

Spider and I had just finished our drawings and plans detailing how our legs would work when Uncle Chet walked in. He was carrying a large bag from the sandwich shop.

"It's noon already?" I asked. "It seems like only an hour has gone by."

"How's it going?" Uncle Chet asked as he placed the bag on the table. I could smell the hot sandwiches, and my stomach growled. I hadn't realized how hungry I was.

"Good," Spider replied. "We finished our designs, and we'll get to work making the legs and connecting them to one of the vacuums this afternoon."

"Great," Uncle Chet said. "I'll leave you guys alone to work. When you're done, I'll see if I can correct those computer problems. Once I do that, the vacuums will be ready to test."

Uncle Chet had lunch with us, and we talked about our plans and all the money we would make. Then, we finished our sandwiches, and Uncle Chet left. Spider and I returned to our work. Thomas Edison was right: a lot of perspiration and work is needed to invent new things. It wasn't like the electronic robot kits we bought at the store, where you follow printed directions. When you invent something like what we were doing, you've got to make your own plans. Sometimes, they don't work out the way you think they will. So, you have to change your plans, which we had to do several times over the afternoon.

Finally, near five o'clock, we had our first vacuum cleaner finished. It was an upright style, and we built retractable legs that folded into the unit, so when it was in operation, the legs wouldn't interfere with the vacuuming. The legs were built from spare pieces of metal and plastic that we found in the storage area. Tiny eyes—sensors—

would tell the vacuum's computer when the legs needed to be deployed to climb over something or to go up and down stairs. The sensors were nothing more than the tiny eyes from remote controlled toys, which we bought at the hobby store for a couple of dollars each. The same sensors would detect the vacuum approaching a wall and enable the unit to turn away.

"Let's try it out," Spider said. "I can't wait to see if it works."

The appliance had been laying on its side on the table. I carefully picked it up and placed it on the floor.

"If this works, we're going to be rich and famous," Spider said.

"And if it works," I said, "I'll never have to vacuum my room ever again."

I placed my fingers on the computer keyboard.

"Here goes," I said, and I typed in the command to turn the unit on.

Things were about to go haywire.

17

I knew something had gone horribly wrong the moment I'd finished typing in the command for the vacuum to start.

First of all, the unit's motor didn't just turn on . . . it *roared*. The motor was so loud that Spider and I both cupped our hands over our ears to drown out the screaming machine.

The vacuum cleaner took off like a dragster, shooting across the room. Just when I thought it was going to smash into the wall, it turned sharply, heading off in another direction.

Spider removed his hands from his ears.

"It's going to hit that table!" he shouted.

But it didn't. Just before it struck the table, the machine turned and darted around it. We leapt to get out of its way as it sped across the room. The senors probably would have detected us in the way and turned, but we weren't taking any chances.

"Something's really wrong!" I shouted over the roaring motor. "I'll shut it down!"

My hands tapped furiously at the computer keyboard. I scrolled down to find the system shutdown command, and I hit the *Enter* key. Instantly, the vacuum cleaner's motor shut down, and the screaming sound faded. The workshop was silent, except for the light drone of rain on the metal roof.

"Wow," Spider said. "We really screwed up somewhere."

"I don't think *we* did," I said. "I think it's a computer problem. Maybe we shouldn't test it out until my uncle fixes it."

"That thing sure was fast," Spider said. "There's no way it would have had the time to pick up any dirt, speeding around like that."

The door to the workshop opened unexpectedly, causing Spider and me to flinch and turn. Uncle Chet strode into the room.

"How are you guys coming along?" he asked.

"We were just testing the vacuum," I replied. "But it's acting crazy. The thing just raced around the room on its own. I think it has to do with the computer."

"Yeah," Spider said. "We've got the legs attached, but we don't know if they work."

"I'll work on the computer glitch tonight," Uncle Chet replied. "You guys come back in the morning, and I promise I'll have the programming error fixed."

Uncle Chet, however, was wrong. He had no problem fixing the computer and reprogramming the machines . . . but that wasn't the trouble.

The trouble was that an accident in the workshop was going to cause a horrific malfunction, allowing the appliances to have dangerous minds of their own.

The rain stopped that night, but in the morning, thick, gray clouds lingered, with even darker ones to the west. Once again, heavy thunderstorms were predicted. Usually, I don't like it when it rains because that means I have to stay inside, especially if there's the threat of lightning. But today, I was looking forward to my job at Uncle Chet's vacuum repair shop. I *wanted* to be inside.

As I did the day before, I rode my bike over to Spider's, and then we rode to my uncle's shop.

This time, however, Spider decided to take Gizmo. The day before, he'd asked Uncle Chet if he could bring Gizmo and let him wander around the warehouse, and my uncle said it was fine. Spider put Gizmo in his backpack and left it open so the cat could see. I thought Gizmo would jump out, but he didn't seem to care at all. In fact, he looked like he was enjoying the ride.

"I thought he might have fun exploring the warehouse," Spider said. "Besides: I don't like to leave him home alone all day. He gets lonely."

"As long as we keep him out of Uncle Chet's secret workshop," I said. "He'd probably get freaked out by the vacuum cleaners running around by themselves."

It started sprinkling by the time we reached the workshop, and the wind was really blowing. Trees bent and swayed, and leaves were torn from their branches and sent hurtling through the air. Gizmo tucked his head into the backpack to avoid the wind and rain.

Inside the shop, Uncle Chet was behind the

counter, talking with a customer. I pointed to the back door, toward the warehouse, and he nodded, indicating for us to go ahead. He continued chatting with the man at the counter as we walked through the shop and exited through the back door.

In the warehouse, Spider put Gizmo on the floor.

"Have fun exploring, pal," he said, and the cat began sniffing the broken appliances.

"Won't he get lost in here?" I said.

"He always comes when he's called," Spider replied. "Besides: where is he going to go? It's not like he can leave the warehouse. He'll be fine, and he'll have fun wandering around."

We continued wading through the maze of old, broken vacuum cleaners until we reached the door to Uncle Chet's secret workshop. My uncle must have been there earlier that morning, because the door was unlocked. It also looked like he'd fixed the top hinge, as the door wasn't loose like it was yesterday.

I pushed it open warily, remembering the previous day when one of the vacuums had attacked us. Today, however, I didn't see anything . . . because the lights were off.

I felt along the wall with my hand, probing for a light switch. When my fingers found one, I flicked it up.

The tubes above made soft tinking sounds and blinked several times before flaring to a full, brilliant bloom, illuminating the room and its contents.

"Whoa," Spider whispered when we saw what was waiting for us. I, too, was shocked. For the moment, all we could do was stare.

All of the vacuum cleaners were standing upright next to the tables. Most of them looked nearly identical, including the one we had been working on the day before. Some were different colors and some were different brands. All were about the same shape and size.

But they all looked like they had mouths with teeth and glaring, watchful eyes. It was as if they were sentries, each one standing guard over the workshop. It looked eerie.

"They almost look like they're alive," Spider whispered. *"Like they're waiting for us."*

"Uncle Chet probably fixed them," I said.

"I did," a voice from behind us said.

We both jumped at the sudden sound. We were still standing in the doorway and hadn't entered the workshop yet. Spider and I turned to see my uncle weaving his way through the forest of old vacuum cleaners, walking toward us.

"I worked late last night," Uncle Chet continued, "and I found a glitch in the central program. I think they're all functioning perfectly now. I reprogrammed the one you two were working on yesterday, but I didn't test the legs. I figured I'd wait until you guys got here. But let me give you a quick demonstration with a different vacuum."

Uncle Chet walked past us, and we followed him to one of the tables.

"I was able to link all of the computers to one mainframe," he said. "That way, I didn't have to reprogram each individual unit. It was quite easy to do, once I discovered the problem. Watch."

Uncle Chet tapped away at the computer keyboard.

"There," he said. "I programmed the vacuum to start in about ten seconds."

I held my breath. I was excited, but I also felt tense and anxious. Nervous.

What if that thing goes crazy? I thought. *What if it goes mad and starts zipping around the room?*

I needn't have worried. The vacuum roared to life, and it sounded like a normal vacuum cleaner. Then, on its own, it began rolling around the room, methodically and controlled, as if it were being pushed by some unseen force.

Which, of course, it was. It was being guided by the computer motherboard Uncle Chet had placed inside of it.

"See?" Uncle Chet said. "All fixed. Just a slight programming error."

"Let's try the one we worked on yesterday," I said. "If the legs work, all we have to do is repeat the process and build mechanical legs for the other vacuums."

While the vacuum cleaner went around the room, we walked to the table where our modified appliance stood. I turned it over on its side, making a few final inspections. Then, I stood it upright.

"All set," I said. "Give it a try."

Uncle Chet tapped at the computer keyboard. After a few seconds, the vacuum cleaner's motor roared to life on its own, and the unit began rolling across the floor. Now there were *two* vacuums at work.

"It needs something to climb over," Spider said. "We need to see if the mechanical legs work."

"Let's just put another vacuum in its path," I said, and I grabbed the handle of one of the units at a nearby table. I pushed it across the room and laid it sideways on the floor, directly in the path of our modified vacuum.

Our invention—the mechanical legs— worked perfectly. For a moment, it looked as if our vacuum was going to bump into the vacuum on its side, but it didn't. Instead, it stopped. Then, four legs stretched out from the base, unfolded, and began to push the vacuum up off the ground like an animal getting to its feet.

"It's working!" Spider said. "It's really working!"

While we watched, the vacuum climbed over the unit that was on its side. Then, the legs retracted, folded in, and the vacuum continued rolling across the floor, hard at work.

"Remarkable!" Uncle Chet said. "You guys are geniuses!"

"We still need to try the vacuum on stairs," I said. "But I think it will work."

"Let's get started on the other vacuums," Spider said. "Once we have them all modified with mechanical legs, we can try them out in our homes."

The modified vacuum made a turn and headed for the open door that led into the warehouse.

"That will be the test," Spider said. "If that vacuum can make it over and around all those other vacuums, it will be a miracle."

The vacuum rolled out the door, turned, and vanished.

Suddenly, there was a ear-splitting yowl, and in a split second, we knew what it was.

"Gizmo!" Spider shouted.

The three of us sprang, sprinting to the door, just in time to see the last of Gizmo's tail vanish into the vacuum cleaner! The cat had been gobbled up by the maniac monster machine!

"Gizmo!" Spider shrieked. *"That thing ate Gizmo!"*

The three of us raced to the machine, which had started to extract its legs so it could climb over other appliances.

"Turn it off!" Spider squealed. He was panicking. "We've got to save Gizmo! We've got to save him!"

I grabbed the appliance's handle and flicked the switch.

"That won't do it!" Uncle Chet said. "I'll have

to turn it off at the terminal!"

My uncle turned and ran, vanishing into his workshop.

"Gizmo!" Spider shouted again. "Hang on, pal! We'll get you out of there!"

We could hear the cat's yowls of fear, sounding strangely hollow from inside the vacuum bag. Spider tried to unzip the bag, but the appliance was jerking crazily, trying to get away. Its legs were now fully retracted, and it was trying to climb over a small shop vacuum that looked a hundred years old.

Uncle Chet succeeded in remotely shutting down the unit, and the droning motor faded until it ceased completely. The appliance stopped, and the only sound we heard was the humming of the other vacuum as it harmlessly went about its work in Uncle Chet's workshop, and the terrified cat squealing and struggling, trapped in the vacuum bag.

"Gizmo! Gizmo!" Spider said as he unzipped the bag. The cat tumbled out, covered with dust and dirt. He was unharmed, but he looked frazzled and confused.

"That was awful," I said.

"Are you all right?" Spider asked as he cradled his cat in his arms.

Uncle Chet rushed into the room.

"Is everything okay?" he asked frantically.

"He's going to be fine," Spider said. "He's just scared."

"Maybe you should rename him," I said. "You could call him Dusty."

"Very funny," Spider said. He wiped some of the fuzz and dirt off Gizmo and returned the cat to the floor.

"Looks like we still have some perfecting to do," I said. "People aren't going to want to buy a vacuum that will eat their pet."

Unfortunately, we would soon find out that pets weren't the only things the vacuums would be after.

We pushed the vacuum back into my uncle's workshop and stood it next to its table. The other vacuum cleaner was still buzzing around the room, and Uncle Chet shut it down by tapping a command on the computer keyboard.

Now that we knew our modifications worked, we were eager to get working on the other vacuums.

"Let's experiment with some legs of different sizes," I suggested. "And let's try some different models, too."

"Great idea," my uncle said. "I'll get to work adding computer motherboards to more units. Maybe we can even try some of the smaller, handheld vacuums. But I'll have to do the work in the front office, so I don't miss any customers."

That was fine with us. Uncle Chet left, leaving us alone to get started. First, we hunted through the warehouse to find parts that we could use to make legs. That was pretty easy to do, because there were so many appliances to choose from. We found dozens of pieces and parts, and we hauled them into the brightly lit workshop, creating a big pile.

We experimented with legs of different sizes, as I thought it might be handy for a vacuum to be able to climb over a coffee table or a small chair. We even tried making legs that would allow a vacuum cleaner to climb over bigger things, like a dining room table or a couch. Problem was, the legs were too cumbersome. When the vacuum was raised that high in the air, it became unbalanced and tipped over.

But the shorter legs functioned great. Spider and I worked right through lunch, building mechanical legs and affixing them to the appliances. Uncle Chet came in once and gave us two handheld vacuums affixed with computer motherboards. It was a bit of a trick to modify the legs for the smaller units, but we got them to work.

I looked at the clock on the wall.

"Wow," I said. "It's almost five o'clock."

"Time sure flew by," Spider said.

We had just finished with the last vacuum. It was one of the handhelds that Uncle Chet had modified earlier that day. After trying it out, we reconnected each vacuum to its battery charger. There were fourteen vacuums in all: twelve upright units and the two smaller handheld vacuums.

"Let's go home for dinner, then come back and try them all out at the same time," I said to Spider. "When we come back, we'll close the door and keep them in my uncle's workshop. If they all work like they're supposed to, they'll climb all over one another without getting stuck."

"Great idea," Spider said. "I can't wait to show people our new invention."

It sounded like a good plan. I mean . . . if we kept all of the vacuums in one room, how could anything go wrong?

Very easily.

But our experiment wasn't simply going to go wrong . . . it was going to be *disastrous*.

We turned off the lights and closed Uncle Chet's workshop door as we left, then made our way through the graveyard of vacuum cleaners.

"Gizmo?" Spider called out. "Here, buddy." We didn't have to wait long. In seconds the cat appeared, and Spider scooped him up. "How's it going, pal?" he said. "Ready to go home?"

We continued walking. Uncle Chet was in the front office, and a customer was just leaving.

"Good news," my uncle said as we walked

into the room. "That guy is going to buy five of my used vacuums."

"Why would someone need five vacuums?" Spider asked.

"He's the manager of an apartment complex, and he wants a vacuum for each person on his cleaning staff. He wanted to save money, so he bought used vacuums instead of new ones. I gave him a great deal. He'll be back later tonight to pick them up."

"We're going to get some dinner," I said, "and we were hoping to come back later and try out all the vacuums."

"I'll be here," my uncle replied. "I'd like to see them in action, too."

Rain was falling lightly as we rode our bikes home. The sky was gray and dark.

"It's been raining for two whole days," Spider said as we pedaled along the sidewalk.

"At least we haven't been caught in any storms," I said. "I can handle a little light rain."

During dinner, Mom and Dad asked how

things were going at Uncle Chet's.

"Great," I said. "Uncle Chet is great to work for."

"Are you getting a lot of cleaning and organizing done for him?" Mom asked.

"Sort of, yeah," I replied. I almost told her about our secret project, but I decided not to. I wanted it to be a surprise.

"Is Chet still as nutty as ever?" Dad asked.

"I guess so," I replied. "But he's really smart. And he's a nice guy, too."

I helped Mom clean the dinner dishes, then I called Spider, telling him I'd be at his house in ten minutes.

"Make sure you take your raincoat," Mom said. "I heard on the news we might get some heavy rains and maybe a thunderstorm this evening."

"I will," I said, and I retrieved my raincoat from the closet where I'd hung it earlier. I put it on. "See you in a couple of hours," I said.

I pedaled to Spider's house, where he was

waiting on his bike. He was wearing his yellow raincoat. Gizmo sat on the porch, watching eagerly.

"You have to stay home, buddy," Spider said to the cat. "There's going to be too much going on, and we don't want you to be a snack for a vacuum cleaner."

As it would turn out, Gizmo wasn't the one we were going to have to worry about . . . because the vacuum cleaners would be more interested in making a snack out of *us*.

It was a good thing I was wearing my raincoat, because halfway to Uncle Chet's shop, the sky opened up and the rain came pouring down. Thunder rumbled in the distance as we rode in and around newly formed puddles.

We pedaled faster. My raincoat kept my hair, head, and the upper portion of my body dry, but it didn't do much for my pants. Thankfully, we weren't too far from the shop, and we made it there before my jeans got soaked.

Uncle Chet greeted us as we hustled our bikes inside.

"It's really coming down out there," he said as Spider and I slipped out of our raincoats. A flash of lightning lit up the sky, followed by a loud crack of thunder.

"Made it just in time," Spider said. "Getting hit by a bolt of lightning would really mess up my night."

"Let's go try out the vacuums," I said

"I'll be back there in a few minutes," Uncle Chet said. "That customer will be here any minute to pick up his vacuums."

Spider and I strode through the shop and into the warehouse, making our way through the wasteland of old vacuums.

"It's going to be cool to see all of the vacuums working at once," I said.

"I can't wait to show people," Spider said. "Think we'll be on television?"

"Probably," I said. "It's not everyday that two kids help create a new invention like this."

We reached my uncle's workshop and opened the door. I flipped the switch and the overhead lights winked on. All of the vacuums were exactly where we'd left them, plugged into their battery chargers.

"Their batteries should be recharged and ready to go," Spider said.

Suddenly, there was an enormous thunderclap and a burst of intense bright light. The overhead fluorescent tubes exploded with a flash of flame and smoke. The computers at each table blew up in a shower of sparks.

Everything went dark, and we could hear shards of glass—pieces of the fluorescent tubes—raining down all around us. Since there were no windows, no light from outside came in. We were in complete darkness.

"Oh, no!" I said. "The building got hit by lightning! Our experiment is ruined!"

At that moment, a vacuum cleaner roared to life, its single light glowing in the darkness like a laser beam.

Then, another vacuum started, followed by another, and another. One of them started moving, and we heard a sharp snapping sound as the cables connecting it to the computer snapped.

"How can this be happening?!?!" Spider asked frantically.

"I don't know," I said, "but I think we'd better get out of here before—"

It was too late. The remaining vacuums roared to life and broke away from their battery chargers, and when all of them began racing toward us, we realized our experiment had gone horribly wrong.

It was total madness.

In the darkness, all we could see were the headlights of the upright vacuums as they screamed toward us like a swarm of fireflies.

"Let's get out of here!" Spider wailed.

We spun and ran, but it was impossible to see where we were going. I tripped over a broken vacuum in the warehouse and crashed to the floor. I heard a loud eruption next to me, and Spider grunted as he, too, tripped and tumbled to the floor.

Behind us, the vacuum cleaners had reached the workshop door. I couldn't believe how loud they were. Each motor whirred like a giant, angry hornet. Their lights were bright white eyes, boring holes through the darkness as they came toward us in the warehouse.

"This is totally crazy!" Spider shrieked, and I caught a glimpse of him as the appliance lights drew closer.

In the darkness, I fumbled around to find something to use as a weapon, maybe an old vacuum or a piece of one. I found a handle and grabbed it, rolling to the side as one of the raging units came at me. I kicked it and knocked it over, only to watch it right itself. Then, ignoring me, it continued its trek through the warehouse, followed by the other vacuums. They screamed past us like race cars at night, dark shadows chasing beams of light through the cluttered warehouse. Some of the vacuums bumped into the broken appliances, but it didn't stop any of them. They continued their crazy charge through the room, following the path that led to the front office.

Finally, the last of the upright vacuums had passed. The two handheld units followed. They didn't have lights, and they blindly bumped into things and careened off one another. It was as if they actually couldn't see, as if having a light would have made a difference.

Regardless, all of the vacuums had passed without further threat to Spider and me.

Uncle Chet, however, wasn't going to be so lucky . . . and when I heard his bloodcurdling scream from the front office, I knew he'd be no match for the marching army of vicious, violent vacuums.

Still holding the broken vacuum handle and brandishing it like a sword, I scrambled to my feet.

"Get up!" I shouted to Spider. Although I couldn't see him, I knew he was nearby. "We've got to save my uncle! There's no way he'll be able to fight those things by himself!"

I stumbled blindly, taking cautious steps as I tried my best to make my way through the nest of old vacuums cluttering the warehouse. Spider was behind me, and every few steps he or I would bump into an old, broken appliance and knock it over.

Ahead of us, we could see dim light pouring through the open door that led to the front office and store. I could hear Uncle Chet hollering and screaming.

"Away!" he shouted. *"Back! Back!"*

Then, he screamed, and I heard a loud crash.

"Faster!" I said as I bumped into yet another broken vacuum and nearly fell.

"We can't go any faster than we are right now!" Spider said. "I can't even see you, and you're right in front of me!"

As we stumbled our way through the darkness, fumbling and blundering along, I could no longer hear my uncle screaming, nor could I hear the angry whine of the vacuum cleaners.

Has he stopped them? I wondered. *How could he stop all of them? They can only be shut down at the computer mainframe, and we watched those things get blown up when the lightning hit.*

Finally, we reached the door. The lights were off, but hazy light from outside came through the window and the front door, which had been propped open.

The vacuums and Uncle Chet were gone.

"What happened to them?" Spider asked.

A knot of fear slowly tightened in my chest as I looked at the open door. The knot grew tighter and tighter, so much so that it felt like a rope was pulled around my rib cage, making it hard to breathe.

Spider looked at the open door.

"You think—" was all he said.

Then, we walked to the open door and looked outside . . . where a nightmare was unfolding.

The good news was that we quickly found Uncle Chet, and he wasn't hurt. The bad news was the scene on the street.

Above, the sky was filled with bulging, swollen storm clouds. They were purple and black, as if they'd been bruised by colliding with one another. Thunder rumbled, and rain fell. The darkening sky cast a sinister pall over what was happening on the ground.

The vacuums were no longer in a pack.

They'd spread out, zipping across the street and into yards and driveways, darting about like gazelles.

And the havoc they were creating! One of the appliances was snapping at the wheel of a car! Another, using the legs Spider and I had invented, had climbed the porch of a house across the street, angrily banging at the front door in an attempt to break it down. One of the handheld vacuums was chasing a terrified squirrel until the animal scampered to the trunk of a tree and bounded up to safety. Even then, the small vacuum tried to scrabble up the tree, rolling over backward, climbing again, and once again falling back. Finally, the machine gave up and screamed across the street.

All around, the air was filled with the shrill screaming of vacuum motors.

"How did they get out here?" I said. I sounded panicky.

"That guy who's buying the vacuum cleaners called," Uncle Chet replied. "He said he would be coming over soon, so I propped the front door open to make it easier for us to carry the vacuums to his truck."

"Now what are we going to do?" Spider asked. He sounded even more panicked than me.

"I'll go back to the computers and shut the machines down," Uncle Chet said. He turned and began to run into his shop.

"You can't!" I said.

Uncle Chet stopped and looked at me, his face a mask of panic and fear.

"Why not?" he asked.

"Because the computers blew up," Spider said. "We saw it happen."

"Yeah," I said. "And besides: the lightning knocked out the electricity."

"Oh, yeah," Uncle Chet said. "The lightning must have caused a malfunction in the battery chargers," he said. "There's no telling what those things will do."

Across the street, one of the upright vacuums was plowing through a garden, gobbling flowers and pulling the roots from the ground as it sucked up the entire plant. The machine actually looked like it was *chewing* the plants as the powerful vacuum yanked them from the soil.

This is crazy! I thought. *This whole thing is way out of hand. There's no way we can stop them. The only thing we can do is hope that nobody gets hurt.*

And that was the precise moment that an old woman came hurrying around the corner. She was carrying a white umbrella . . . and walking a small, brown Chihuahua on a black leather leash.

The dog spotted one of the vacuums on the other side of the street. It stopped walking and turned its head curiously. A low throaty rumble came from his chest.

The vacuum cleaner spotted the dog.

The old woman saw the bizarre scene on the street. She stopped, too, her jaw hanging open in disbelief as vacuums raced across yards and driveways.

The little dog growled and took a step

backward . . . but it was already too late. The upright vacuum tore across the street, motor running, heading straight for the Chihuahua!

27

The old woman didn't have time to pick up her dog or try to get away. She didn't even have time to scream. And, although the little dog tried to run off, he couldn't because he was attached to the leash.

In seconds, the vacuum was upon the little Chihuahua. The woman dropped the leash and the helpless dog yelped once before falling victim to the hungry mouth of the attacking appliance. In the next moment, the dog was gone, leaving only the black leash dangling from the base of the vacuum. Then, the unit sucked in the leash like a child slurping up a strand of spaghetti.

The old woman was grief-stricken and stunned. She stood on the sidewalk, frozen in shock and disbelief, still holding the umbrella over her head. I felt horrible.

"We've got to help!" I shouted.

I snapped my head both ways to make sure there were no cars coming, then rushed across the street. My uncle and Spider followed.

The vacuum had already started to race away, but I caught up to it. I grabbed the handle, but was completely surprised when the machine wrestled from my grasp. It was as if it was a wild animal, not an inanimate electrical appliance.

Still, I persisted, chasing the vacuum down the sidewalk. Uncle Chet appeared by my side and together we dove and tackled the raging appliance.

Now, more than ever, the machine behaved like a crazed, wild animal. It twisted and turned, its powerful intake acting more like a mouth than a vacuum cleaner base. Once, it grabbed my hand and the powerful suction nearly sucked in my entire arm. I had to pull with all my might to work it free and was surprised to see dark red indentations—bite marks—on my wrist.

"The thing's alive!" I shrieked as I leapt away.

Uncle Chet held the handle firmly with both hands, still trying to subdue the vacuum. Finally, he was able to put his foot on the base and twist the handle. There was a loud snap as the handle broke. Still, the base of the unit flopped around like a fish out of water until my uncle was able to remove the plastic casing from the handle and pop out the rechargeable battery.

Instantly, the broken unit stopped moving. The vacuum bag, however, was still alive, and I realized that it wasn't the appliance itself, but the old woman's Chihuahua. Uncle Chet reached down and unzipped the bag. The little brown dog spilled out, still connected to the leash. He was shaking and looked horrified.

"Snoopy!" the old woman cried. "Oh,

Snoopy! You're alive!"

The Chihuahua scampered to the old woman, and she scooped him up with one arm and held him tightly.

"You're all right, Snoopy," the old woman said. "You're safe. You'll be all right."

I was relieved, but I still felt horrible. It had been our fault that the dog was swallowed by the vacuum cleaner. The animal hadn't been hurt, but he was very frightened, as was the poor old woman.

"Let's chase them down!" Uncle Chet said. "We'll have to remove the battery pack from each one."

The air sizzled with the revving sounds of the high-pitched vacuum cleaner motors. Thunder rumbled in the distance. A light rain continued to fall, and I realized for the first time that I was completely soaked.

Meanwhile, the vacuum that had climbed the porch was still battering itself against the door. Suddenly, the door opened, and a man appeared.

"What on earth is—"

That was all he had time to say. The vacuum cleaner reared back on its four mechanical legs, lunged forward, and tackled the man. He fell backward with the crazed machine on top of him, and all we could hear were his painful screams and pleas for mercy as the horrible appliance prepared to make a meal out of him.

Not a single word was spoken as Uncle Chet, Spider, and I raced to help the man. His screams were ear-piercing, louder than the vacuum cleaner, and we knew he wouldn't last long. I wasn't sure what the appliances were capable of doing, but I was certain of two things: they were vicious, and they were ruthless. Uncle Chet had made their wire brushes like rows of sharp teeth so the vacuums would have more power to clean. Without knowing it, he'd created deadly killing machines . . . and now it appeared that a vacuum was about to claim its first victim.

My uncle was the first to reach the man. He bounded through the doorway, followed by me, then Spider.

The scene in the house was horrible. On the floor, the vacuum cleaner was poised above the man, supported by its four mechanical legs. The base of the unit—the appliance's head—was brutally striking at the man's chest. His shirt was being sucked into the vacuum while the man was frantically trying to push it away. Above him stood the man's wife, hitting the vacuum with a broom. It was almost comical, and if I had been watching the scene on television or reading it in a book, I would have laughed out loud.

But not now. This was serious. The man was in danger, and the woman was horrified. This wasn't a joke, and it certainly wasn't a laughing matter.

Uncle Chet dove forward, knocking the vacuum cleaner sideways. It crashed to the floor, upending a coffee table. Magazines and a ceramic mug flew to the floor. The mug made a loud thud as it hit, and ceramic pieces skittered about as it shattered.

The woman continued swinging, battering the vacuum with her broom. The man, freed from the clutches of the attacking appliance, leapt to his feet. His shirt was torn open, but he didn't appear to be injured.

"What on earth?!?!" he shouted as he backed away.

On the floor, Uncle Chet was struggling with the writhing vacuum cleaner, rolling and thrashing around like he was wrestling with an alligator.

Meanwhile, the woman continued to beat the unit with the broom.

"Take that!" she said as the machine took another blow. *Whack!* "And that!" *Whack!* "That, too!" *Whack!*

Spider and I sprang.

"Break its legs!" I shouted.

I grabbed one and twisted, surprised at how

firmly attached it was. Spider and I had designed the legs to not only support the vacuum, but also give it the added strength it would need to climb stairs. I quickly found it difficult to simply break off one of the legs.

Seeing me struggle, Spider grabbed the leg. "Pull!" he shouted.

Finally, the leg snapped, and the vacuum let out an eerie, loud whine. It was creepy. It was as if the appliance was alive, that it actually felt pain.

That's not possible, I thought. *It's a vacuum cleaner. It's made out of metal and plastic. It can't feel anything, and it's certainly not alive.*

Uncle Chet rolled over, pinning the machine to the floor. The woman stopped swinging her broom and held it before her like she was brandishing a sword.

"The battery casing!" Uncle Chet shouted. "Get the casing open and pull the battery!"

Spider found the plastic cover and popped it open. The battery fell out, and the effect was instant. The vacuum's motor died, and the loud whirring quickly faded.

"What's going on?" the man asked. He'd backed all the way to the wall and stood there, terrified. "I've lived in Gainesville for forty years, and I've never seen anything like this. Why did that thing attack me?"

"We don't have time to explain," Uncle Chet said as he got to his knees and climbed to his feet. "We still have twelve more of these things to stop. Are you all right?"

The man looked down and inspected himself. "Just a torn shirt," he replied.

"Sorry about that," I said.

"Don't worry about it," the man replied. "I feel lucky to be alive."

And that's when it really hit me.

This is like a Frankenstein movie gone bad, I thought. *We created not one, but fourteen little monsters. Those things really are vicious and could seriously hurt someone . . . or worse.*

Even from inside the house, we could hear the sound of vacuums screaming and zipping around the neighborhood.

Then, we heard something else:

A police siren.

Things were about to get *really* serious.

Spider, Uncle Chet, and I hurried to the open front door. The man and woman followed, and the five of us scanned the neighborhood.

Parked in the street was a blue and white police truck. It had a thin bar of lights on top, flashing red and blue. Big gold letters on the side of the truck read *Animal Control*.

And in front of the truck, a vacuum cleaner had stopped, facing the vehicle like a bull challenging a bullfighter.

"That's an animal control officer," Spider said. "The dog catcher. What's *he* going to do?"

As if in response, the door of the truck opened, and a man in a gray uniform and gray hat slipped out. He hustled to the back of his truck, reached inside, and pulled out a long pole with a rope at the end. The rope formed a loop—a noose of sorts—used to catch stray animals.

"He's not going to be able to catch one of those things with that," Spider said. "Those vacuums are too fast."

"And too strong," I said.

"He might be able to," Uncle Chet said, "if he can get that loop over the handle and wrestle the vacuum to the ground."

The loud, high-pitched whine of vacuum cleaners echoed through the neighborhood. I watched one of the handheld appliances scurry across the street like a mad rat. A few houses away, an upright vacuum had climbed on top of a car.

And in other homes along the street, people

were peering out their doors and windows in shock and amazement. No one could believe what they were seeing.

In the street, the vacuum remained frozen, its motor revving as if it were preparing to strike. The animal control officer was approaching cautiously, extending the long pole in front of him, dangling the noose closer and closer to the upright. The scene reminded me of a matador challenging a bull in an arena.

"I think he's going to do it," the man behind me said.

"You don't know what they're capable of," I replied. "If that guy isn't careful—"

Without warning, another vacuum zipped out from the other side of the truck. It had been stalking the officer, unseen, waiting for the perfect moment to strike, the perfect moment for an ambush.

And that perfect moment was *now*.

Surprised by the new attacker, the animal control officer spun. This prompted the vacuum in the street to surge forward, confusing the man. Both appliances hit him at the same time, sending the long pole flying and knocking the officer off his feet.

Once again, the three of us raced to the rescue. Even the man and the woman came along to help.

The officer was kicking and thrashing, trying

to push the vacuums away. The appliances were relentless, attacking like two snarling lions.

"Remember!" Uncle Chet shouted. "Get the battery casings off and pull the batteries out! The vacuums won't work without them!"

Spider and I pulled one vacuum off the animal control officer. While I held it down, Spider kicked the battery casing cover. The swift blow broke the plastic, the battery fell out, and the appliance died.

Uncle Chet was trying to wrestle the other vacuum off the officer. The man and his wife were helping: the man had ahold of the vacuum bag and was pulling it sideways, while the woman beat the appliance with her broom. I thought her actions were useless . . . until she connected with the handle and popped off the plastic casing. Uncle Chet saw this and quickly pulled the battery from the unit.

The rain fell around us as the animal control officer got to his feet, staring down in disbelief at the two motionless vacuums in the wet street.

"I'm not sure if I'm even going to call this one in," he said. "I don't think anyone in the department is going to believe me."

"There are ten more machines on the loose," my uncle said. "If we don't stop them, there's no telling what they'll do."

"Ten more?!?!" the officer said. "Who's responsible for this?"

"We are," I said sheepishly, and I looked at Spider.

"Me, too," my uncle said. "We didn't mean for this to happen. They're experimental vacuums. There was a lightning strike at my workshop, and that caused all of the appliances to malfunction."

It was then that I realized that not only had our experiment gone completely out of control, but we'd created a dangerous situation for everyone in our neighborhood. It was our fault. We could get arrested and thrown in jail.

But I would worry about that later. I was more concerned with stopping the vacuums that were still on the loose, wondering how we were going to round them up and stop them before someone got hurt.

And what if a couple of them get away? I thought. Sure, their batteries will run down sooner or later. In the meantime, what kind of damage will they cause. Will anyone get hurt?

But while I was thinking about how we were going to hunt down the vacuum cleaners, it never really occurred to me that the vacuum cleaners might band together and do some hunting on their own . . . *for us!*

Along the street, several people emerged from their homes. They moved slowly, warily, unsure and uncertain as they gazed around the neighborhood. Uncle Chet raised his arms and made a pushing motion, urging them to stay away.

"Go back," he said. "Go back into your houses. It's too dangerous out here right now. We'll let you know when it's safe to come out."

The people turned around and went back into their homes. Most of them went to a window where they could look outside and watch what was going on.

"I'll radio for some help," the animal control officer said. He picked up the long pole and hurried back to his truck, and I could hear him talking on his radio.

"Let's stick together," Uncle Chet said. "Together, we stand a better chance of stopping them."

"We're going inside while we still can," the man said. He and his wife, who was still wielding her broom, scurried off and went back into their home.

"Let's take them on one at a time," Spider said.

"Maybe we should just wait until more police arrive," I suggested.

Just then, the animal control officer emerged from his truck. He looked grim.

"Well, it was just as I thought," he said. "They don't believe me at the department. They said they'll send a car, but it will be a while. The storm and the power outage have caused a lot of damage around the city, and most officers are busy with more important problems."

"This is pretty important if you ask me," I said.

The animal control officer shrugged. "I agree with you, but we're on our own right now."

My uncle explained to the animal control officer how to stop the vacuums by pulling out the batteries.

"That seems like a good idea," the uniformed man said, "but we've got to find them first."

"Wait a minute, guys," I said. "Listen."

We paused for a moment.

"I don't hear anything," Spider said.

"That's what I mean," I replied. "There's nothing to hear. I don't hear a single vacuum cleaner."

We listened, straining to hear the whine of a motor, but all we heard was the faint sound of traffic from a busy street a few blocks away.

"That means we're going to have to hunt for them," Uncle Chet said. "They could be scattered over several blocks. We're going to have to hurry."

Spider's face suddenly went ashen. His eyes widened, and his jaw fell.

"No, we won't," he said. "We won't have to look for them." He raised his arm and pointed up the street. "They're looking for *us.*"

I turned and saw the most bizarre scene I'd ever seen in my entire life.

Coming toward us, very slowly, were the remaining uprights and two handheld vacuum cleaners. They'd spread out, filling the street, and were swaggering toward us like cowboys in the old west preparing for a gunfight.

It was time for a showdown.

My mind drifted, and I imagined what the scene looked like from the air: the black rooftops and dark gray street, both shiny from the rain. The shimmering leaves on the trees, cars in driveways. At one end of the street, a line of gangster vacuums moving slowly toward four people standing in front of a blue and white truck with red and blue flashing lights on top. In my mind, it really *was* a movie.

I shook the thought away and stared at the

vacuums that were slowly rolling toward us. It was strange: we could hear their motors, but they were faint, only growing louder as they approached.

And the only thing I could think of at that moment were two simple words.

We're outnumbered.

"Are those things remote controlled?" the animal control officer asked.

"They used to be," Uncle Chet replied. "They've each got their own individual computer motherboard. They're programmed and specially designed to clean houses, but something's gone wrong. The lightning wrecked the main computer, and there's no way to remotely shut the vacuums off."

"Well, there's an easy way to fix this," the animal control officer said. He returned to his truck, slipped inside, and closed the door. Spider, Uncle Chet, and I stepped back as the truck moved forward.

Of course, I thought. *That's going to be the best way to stop them. He's simply going to mow them down with his police truck.*

Unfortunately, it would be a violent, final end to our experiment. Oh, we still had the vacuums that we'd pulled the batteries out of. I was sure that Uncle Chet could fix those, so they wouldn't go crazy and attack people. But we'd worked hard on all those appliances, and now they were going to be ruined.

But at least no one else is going to get attacked or hurt, I thought.

The truck picked up speed as it moved toward the line of vacuum cleaners. As if expecting the vehicle, the appliances split up. Several of the units scooted away, and their mechanical legs emerged as they reached the curb and climbed out of the street like giant insects on bony, metal limbs.

There were several loud crunches as the truck rolled over some of the appliances. As the vehicle mowed them down, our vacuums became nothing more than broken pieces of plastic, metal, and wires. Just for good measure, the animal control officer stopped the truck, then backed over the appliances once more . . . just to make sure they weren't going to be a threat. It was a quick way to eliminate most of the vacuums.

Still, there were three vacuums that were loose. One was a handheld, and it scrabbled up a driveway and ducked into some bushes like a frightened rabbit. The other two uprights were close to one another on the opposite side of the street, in a yard. Both were heading around the side of the house, and there was no way for the animal control officer to get them with his truck.

"Let's get the smaller unit first," Uncle Chet said. "Then, we'll go get the last two upright machines."

We sprinted over the curb and up the driveway to a row of thick green bushes growing near the house. I could hear the handheld unit whirring, but I couldn't see it.

On the street, the animal control officer was getting out of his truck. He retrieved the long pole with the rope and set out after the two uprights. I remember thinking that maybe it wasn't such a good idea for him, that he should wait so the three of us could help him out, as four against two were much better odds.

But I quickly forgot about him. Instead, I concentrated on the smaller vacuum crawling around within the bushes.

"I think I see it, right there," Spider said as he pulled a branch away.

I leaned over his shoulder just as the small unit shot out like a rocket, missing my foot by mere inches. The thing had literally used its mechanical legs to leap into the air. Spider and I jumped and spun, surprised by the speed and power of the handheld.

Uncle Chet, however, was faster. In one swift motion, he raised his foot and brought it down on the vacuum. Plastic crunched, and several pieces broke off. The motor died instantly, and the appliance now lay in the grass, looking exactly like what it was: a broken, handheld vacuum cleaner. Nothing more.

"Now let's go help that guy and get those other two vacuum cleaners," Uncle Chet said. "Then, we'll have to get started cleaning up the mess we made."

But when we heard the officer's screams pierce the air, I wondered the same thing my uncle and Spider wondered.

Was it already too late?

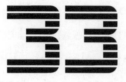

The screams from the animal control officer brought the three of us to a full run. Our shoes smacked the wet pavement as we raced across the street past the blue and white truck, across the lawn, between two houses, and into a backyard. There, we found the animal control officer backed up against a tree while the last two vacuum cleaners lunged at him. The uniformed man kept trying to dart to the side to get away, but each time he did, one of the appliances was faster, heading him off and forcing him back against the tree. He even tried kicking the units, but they never lost their balance.

"We need to distract them!" Uncle Chet said. "Let's see if we can get their attention long enough for him to get away!"

We approached quickly but cautiously, fanning out around the animal control officer and the two vacuum cleaners like wolves. The appliances continued to hound him. The uniformed man kept trying to get away, but he wasn't having much luck. The vacuums were relentless in their attack.

Uncle Chet stopped.

"Okay," he said, "on the count of three, we charge. Knock the vacuums to the ground and keep them pinned while we get the batteries out."

I shot a quick glance behind me. In the house, a man, woman, and two kids were watching what was going on in their backyard, their faces displaying looks of utter disbelief and confusion.

"One," Uncle Chet said, and I returned my attention to the two vacuums attacking the officer.

"Two—"

I looked at Spider, and he looked at me.

"Three!" Uncle Chet shouted.

We rushed the appliances. One of them tried to get away, but Uncle Chet grabbed the handle and wrestled it to the ground. Spider and I grabbed the other one. Now, you would think that it wouldn't be difficult to tackle a vacuum cleaner, but you have to remember: these weren't ordinary household appliances. Something had happened to them when the lightning struck, something had brought them to life, had altered their computer motherboards. They really *did* seem to have minds of their own.

Uncle Chet was struggling with the vacuum he'd brought down. The machine was wriggling and fighting and trying to get at him while my uncle was trying to get at the casing to pop out the battery. The animal control officer came to his aid, stepping on the unit's handle until Uncle Chet was finally able to subdue the vacuum long enough to remove the battery. The machine fell silent.

Spider and I continued to struggle with the vacuum we'd taken on, but Uncle Chet and the officer quickly came to our aid. The vacuum had drawn Spider's foot into its mouth-like intake, and Spider yelped as the machine tried to take a bite of his foot. Uncle Chet kicked the machine and the casing broke open, expelling the square battery. The vacuum's motor whirred to a stop, and the noise died. The only sound we heard was the distant hum of traffic on the street a few blocks away.

Spider and I remained in the wet grass, looking at the two lifeless vacuum cleaners.

We're going to have a lot of explaining to do, I thought. Which was going to be difficult, as I didn't really have any idea what had really gone wrong or why. All we'd done was create some experimental vacuums that were supposed to work on their own. We never expected them to come to life and create the problems they did.

But it was over. All fourteen vacuum cleaners had been stopped. Whatever had gone wrong, we'd been able to stop the appliances before anyone had been hurt. Sure, some people had been pretty scared. I felt bad for the old woman and her dog. They'd been terrified.

And the man and the woman. The man's shirt had been torn, but, thankfully, he hadn't been hurt. I'll never forget the woman, swinging her broom, bringing it down again and again on the vacuum. Looking back, *that* was funny.

And everything turned out fine. The animal control officer took our names and jotted down some notes. When I asked him if we were going to get into trouble, he just smiled and shook his head.

"Like I told you," he said, "nobody's going to believe this. Besides: no one was injured. Just be sure to clean up the pieces of the broken vacuums."

And with that, he got into his truck and drove off.

"Let's go back to the warehouse and get my

work van," Uncle Chet said. "We can load all of the broken vacuums inside."

We were only two blocks from his shop, so it took us only a couple of minutes to get there. We were talking about what could have possibly happened to make the appliances come to life when Spider suddenly stopped and grabbed my wrist. His other arm shot out, pointing ahead of us.

In front of Uncle Chet's shop, several upright vacuum cleaners stood at attention, waiting for us.

34

Our shock and terror quickly turned to relief when we saw a man emerge from the shop. He began loading the vacuums into a waiting truck.

"It's only my customer," Uncle Chet said as we began walking again. "He's come to pick up the vacuum cleaners that he bought. In all the excitement, I forgot he was going to be here."

I looked at Spider, and we both shook our heads and smiled, glad that we didn't have any more vacuum cleaners to worry about.

I was eager to begin repairing the vacuums and continuing with our experiments, but it wasn't going to happen for a while. The lightning strike completely destroyed all of Uncle Chet's computer mainframes. They had been totally cooked and fried to a crisp, and there was nothing salvageable. Which was too bad, because a couple of years had gone into his project. Uncle Chet said it would be a while before he could build a new computer designed to connect to the vacuums. Still, it was exciting to think about continuing our work. I knew that once we got started again, our project would be a success.

I continued working for Uncle Chet in the following weeks, helping him repair vacuum cleaners. And I cleaned and organized his warehouse, too, which was a big help. It made things easier to find, which made our work go much faster. I saved the money I earned and bought some really cool electronic kits.

One week in October, I got excused from school and traveled with Mom to Las Vegas, where she attended a convention. It was just her and me, because Dad was working on some big design project and couldn't get away. Andrew couldn't go, because he wasn't doing very well in school, and Dad said he needed to stay and spend time getting his grades up.

We stayed with Mom's sister in Henderson, which is a city southeast of Las Vegas. During the day when Mom was at the convention, my aunt drove me all around to see the sights. The whole Las Vegas area is really cool, especially at night. The city comes alive with bright, colorful lights, and there are all kinds of shows and theaters. One night we went to see a magic show, and it was awesome!

One afternoon after lunch I walked to Discovery Park, which is only a few blocks from my aunt's house. Discovery Park is cool. There's a playground, a baseball field, basketball courts . . . even volleyball and tennis courts. There is also a big field where a boy and a girl about my age were tossing a softball back and forth. The girl made a wild throw, and the ball took an odd bounce and landed right in my hands. The boy who had tried to catch it jogged toward me, and I tossed the ball to him.

"Thanks," he said. "Wanna play? We have an extra glove."

I've never played much softball, but at the time, it seemed like it might be fun. I had nothing else to do.

"Sure," I said, "but I'm not very good."

"You can't be any worse than my sister," he said with a grin. "I'm Devon. That's my sister, Hannah, over there. I'll go get you the glove."

Devon jogged over to a backpack beneath a tree and returned with a beat-up leather glove.

"It's kind of old, but it'll work," Devon said.

We played catch for a while, and I was proud that I didn't make a fool out of myself with any horrible throws or missed catches. After a while, Hannah announced that she was going home. Devon and I threw the ball back and forth for a few more minutes. Then, we took a break, sitting down at a picnic table.

"You don't throw too bad," Devon said.

"Softball isn't my specialty," I replied. "But I play once in a while with some friends in Virginia."

"Virginia?" Devon asked. "Is that where you live?"

"Yes," I said with a nod. "My mom has a convention in Las Vegas this week, and I took the week off from school to come out with her. We're staying at my aunt's house here in Henderson."

We got talking about hobbies, and I told Devon about some of the robots I've built. He listened, fascinated, but he also looked confused.

"What's the matter?" I asked.

"Oh, nothing, really," Devon said. "It's just that I've never met many girls that are interested in electronics or robotics."

"I am," I said. "And I'm pretty good at making things. In fact—"

I hesitated. *Should I tell him about the vacuum cleaners?* I wondered. *Should I tell him what had happened?*

"What?" he asked. "What were you going to say?"

"Nothing," I said, deciding not to tell him about our crazy experiment gone wrong. "We just had a crazy thing happen with our last project."

"Let me tell you," Devon said, "nothing could be crazier than what just happened to me."

"What's that?" I said, glad that he hadn't pressed me for more information.

"A nightmare came to life," Devon replied. "It was the scariest thing I've ever experienced."

"What do you mean?" I asked.

"I mean just what I said," he answered. "A nightmare came to life. It was real."

"How could that happen?" I asked.

"I asked myself that same question," Devon replied. "It all started with a school assignment."

He continued, and I listened. When he had finished, I had to admit: what had happened to Devon was ten times more horrifying than what had happened to me.

Next:

AMERICAN
CHILLERS
AMERICA'S #1 SERIES FOR MAXIMUM CHILLS!

#31: The Nevada Nightmare Novel

Continue on for a FREE preview!

It was a dark and stormy night in Henderson, Nevada.

In my bedroom, I stared at the words on the computer screen, and read them out loud.

"It was a dark and stormy night in Henderson, Nevada."

That was how my story was to begin. It was a homework assignment. Everyone in our class had to write a spooky Halloween story, and it had to start with that sentence.

It was a dark and stormy night in Henderson, Nevada.

Why? Because our teacher, Mr. Harper, said that it would help our creativity. He said that all of our stories would be very different and unique, even though each student began the exercise with the same sentence.

And Henderson, Nevada, is where I live, of course. It's where I go to school. I'm a fifth-grader at Vandenburg Elementary. Henderson is a city about ten miles southeast of Las Vegas . . . and I think just about everybody's heard of Las Vegas. It's a fun city.

But Henderson is just as much fun. I have a lot of great friends, and there are some great parks nearby, including Discovery Park, which is only a few blocks from where we live. The weather gets really hot in the summer, but it cools off during the winter months. Still, we don't get any snow because it doesn't get cold enough. Sometimes, I wish we would have a snowstorm. I think it would be fun to build a snowman or have a snowball fight with friends.

But I couldn't think about that now. Right now, I had to think about my homework assignment, which was writing a story. I already had the first sentence, of course, but I didn't know what to write about after that.

A ghost story? I thought. *A haunted house? A boy wizard? A fantasy world filled with dragons?*

I had so many options, so many directions I could go, that I found it confusing to even begin. Mr. Harper had told us that writing a book, even a short story, can be difficult. He told us to work hard and to let our imaginations guide us.

Well, my imagination wasn't guiding me anywhere. I just sat at the desk in my bedroom, staring at the computer screen, blank except for that single, short phrase. The little black cursor taunted me as it blinked at the end of the sentence.

It was a dark and stormy night in Henderson, Nevada.

But the weird part? It really *was* a dark and stormy night. It was October, and a chilly wind was blowing, rain was falling, and lightning had been flashing for the past couple of hours. One thunderclap was so loud that it shook the house.

My sister, Hannah, came to my bedroom door. "Devon," she said, "Mom says to shut off your computer until the storm passes."

"Tell her I will," I said.

Using the mouse, I moved the cursor to click the *Off* button, but it was too late. A sudden, bright flash lit up my bedroom window, and at the exact same time an enormous thunderclap exploded. Simultaneously, my bedroom light went out . . . and sparks shot out of the electrical outlets!

2

The power came back on several hours later. Lightning had struck an electrical transformer in front of our house, causing a strong power surge and knocking out power for several blocks.

But the really bad news?

The surge of electricity fried a bunch of our household appliances, including the stereo, microwave, television . . . and my computer. Dad said that he was sure that our insurance would pay to have everything replaced, but that didn't help me at the moment. I really needed to get started on my story for school, but now I had nothing to write with. The computer in my bedroom was the only one in the house. Even though it was a little old and I couldn't use it to play any games, it still worked well enough for my homework assignments.

"I guess you're just going to have to write your story the old-fashioned way," Mom said.

"How's that?" I asked.

"With a pen and paper," she replied.

I frowned. I didn't have any trouble with writing on paper, but I was getting faster and faster at the computer keyboard. I liked the feeling of the keys under my finger, and I liked the way the letters and words came out all neat and crisp when printed on white paper.

But I had two weeks before the story needed to be handed in, so I had plenty of time. I could always use a computer at school or at the public library if I needed to. And besides: the story didn't have to be very long. Mr. Harper had told us to keep it around three pages.

But I was still stuck.

What am I going to write about? I thought, as I lay back in bed. I wanted my story to be different than anyone else's. I knew that most of my classmates would be writing about ghosts or haunted houses or vampires, and there was nothing wrong with that.

But I really want my story to be different, I thought. *What could I write that would be different, and really, really great?*

As it would turn out, I wouldn't have to worry about getting an idea for a really great story. What I would have to worry about was a nightmare . . . not something in my sleep, but a real, live nightmare that came to me while I was awake.

But the most horrifying part? I had no control over the nightmare—and that why things got way out of hand.

The morning after the storm, Hannah and I rode our bikes around the block to see what other damage the storm had done. Tree branches had been snapped off, littering the yards. One of them was big, and it landed on a car. The hood had a big dent in it, and the windshield was smashed. I saw a few trucks that belonged to the power company, their yellow lights flashing.

"We're lucky we didn't get a tornado," Hannah said. "This is bad enough as it is."

Looping around the next block, we saw a man tacking an orange cardboard sign to an electrical pole. When he was finished, he back off, inspected his work, then walked off.

"Garage Sale," Hannah said, reading the sign out loud. "15897 Bobtail Circle. Today and Tomorrow Only."

"Wanna go?" I asked. "It's only a couple of blocks away."

"Sure," Hannah replied.

I liked going to garage sales. Sometimes, you can find some really cool stuff. Last summer at a garage sale, I found a box of comic books for two dollars! I couldn't believe it. I looked on the Internet, and some of the older comics were worth as much as ten dollars. I didn't sell them, though. I figured the longer I held onto them, the more valuable they would be. Maybe they would be worth a fortune when I got older.

We rode our bikes along the sidewalk. In several places, we had to swerve around tree branches that had fallen. After rounding a corner, we came to a big tree that had fallen, blocking our way. We slowed, and I looked behind us.

"There aren't any cars coming," I said. "Let's go around."

We carefully rode into the empty street, and I looked over my shoulder again just to be sure there weren't any vehicles coming from behind us.

Unfortunately, the tree was blocking our view of a driveway, and we had no idea there was a truck backing out at that very moment.

Hannah screamed. We hadn't been traveling very fast, and that's what saved us both from getting hit by the truck. Our brakes shrieked as our bikes came to a halt only inches from the vehicle.

The driver, hearing Hannah's scream, stomped on the brakes. The vehicle jerked to a halt. He got out and hurried around the back of the truck. He looked panicky and scared.

"Are you kids all right?" he asked.

"Yeah," Hannah said. "We didn't see you."

"I didn't see you, either," the man said. "Not with that big tree in the way. You sure you're both all right?"

"Yeah," I said. "We're fine."

"Okay," the man said with a smile. "That storm sure was a doozy, wasn't it?"

"It sure was," I replied.

The man got back into his truck and waited for us to pass.

"That was close," Hannah said as we rode back onto the sidewalk and continued down the block.

Up ahead, we saw another orange sign for the garage sale. A dark arrow was beneath it.

"There it is," I said, and we coasted to a stop at the driveway.

There were a few cars lining the street, and a few people milling about in the driveway. There was a two-car garage attached to the house, and the big door had been rolled up. Three big folding tables had been set up, and they were filled with all sorts of things: old compact discs, shoes, clothes, games, lamps, tools, and more.

"These people must have been saving this stuff for years," Hannah whispered. *"How did they fit all this junk in their house?"*

I snickered. There really was a lot of stuff, and it didn't look like it would all fit into the garage and the house put together.

"Feel free to look around," a man said, and I recognized him as the guy who had put up the sign.

"Thanks," I replied.

Hannah and I wandered around the tables, looking for anything of interest. Mostly, it just seemed like a lot of old junk. Still, some people had found things they thought would be useful, and they carried various items as they pawed through the tables.

Hannah was looking at some collectible dolls, and walked into the garage, where more tables were lined up, and a shelf filled with books on the far wall. A handwritten sign read:

All Books - 25 Cents

Can't beat that, I thought, and I walked to the shelf. I really like to read, and I thought I might find a book that I like.

There were a lot of westerns, which I didn't really care for. And romance books. Yuck. I found a science fiction book that looked cool, along with another book about fog phantoms in Florida.

I was just about to dig out fifty cents to pay for the two books, when another book caught my eye. It looked old, and it didn't have a title on the spine or on the cover.

I picked it up, unaware that I was about to make a terrifying discovery that would turn my world upside down.

ABOUT THE AUTHOR

Johnathan Rand is the author of more than 65 books, with well over 4 million copies in print. Series include **AMERICAN CHILLERS**, **MICHIGAN CHILLERS**, **FREDDIE FERNORTNER**, **FEARLESS FIRST GRADER**, and **THE ADVENTURE CLUB**. He's also co-authored a novel for teens (with Christopher Knight) entitled **PANDEMIA**. When not traveling, Rand lives in northern Michigan with his wife and three dogs. He is also the only author in the world to have a store that sells only his works: **CHILLERMANIA!** is located in Indian River, Michigan. Johnathan Rand is not always at the store, but he has been known to drop by frequently. Find out more at:

www.americanchillers.com

ATTENTION YOUNG AUTHORS!
DON'T MISS

JOHNATHAN RAND'S

AUTHOR QUEST®

THE DEFINITIVE WRITER'S CAMP
FOR SERIOUS YOUNG WRITERS©

If you want to sharpen your writing skills, become a better writer, and have a blast, Johnathan Rand's Author Quest is for you!

Designed exclusively for young writers, Author Quest is 4 days/3 nights of writing courses, instruction, and classes at Camp Ocqueoc, nestled in the secluded wilds of northern lower Michigan. Oh, there are lots of other fun indoor and outdoor activities, too . . . but the main focus of Author Quest is about becoming an even better writer! Instructors include published authors and (of course!) Johnathan Rand. No matter what kind of writing you enjoy: fiction, non-fiction, fantasy, thriller/horror, humor, mystery, history . . . this camp is designed for writers who have this in common: they LOVE to write, and they want to improve their skills!

For complete details and an application, visit:

www.americanchillers.com

JOIN THE FREE AMERICAN CHILLERS FAN CLUB!

It's easy to join . . . and best of all, it's FREE!
Find out more today by visiting:

WWW.AMERICANCHILLERS.COM

And don't forget to browse the on-line superstore, where you can order books, hats, shirts, and lots more cool stuff!

All AudioCraft books are proudly printed, bound, and manufactured in the United States of America, utilizing American resources, labor, and materials.

USA